HE
SENT FORTH
A RAVEN

By Elizabeth Madox Roberts

THE HAUNTED MIRROR

A BURIED TREASURE

THE GREAT MEADOW

JINGLING IN THE WIND

MY HEART AND MY FLESH

THE TIME OF MAN

UNDER THE TREE (verse)

Elizabeth Madox Roberts

HE
SENT FORTH
A RAVEN

New York   Mcmxxxv

Published by The Viking Press

FIRST PUBLISHED MARCH 1935

DISTRIBUTED IN CANADA BY THE MACMILLAN COMPANY OF CANADA, LTD.
PRINTED IN THE UNITED STATES OF AMERICA BY QUINN AND BODEN

HE

SENT FORTH

A RAVEN

I

STONER DRAKE made a vow, solemnly spoken, weighted with passionate words. If Joan Drake should die he would never set his foot on God's earth again.

STONER DRAKE, married first to Helen Ware, married later to Joan Lansdown, this marriage being made in 1899. It was when Joan sickened as if for death that he spoke his vow. He was forty-five years old at this time, Joan dying 1901.

When he had spoken thus, his friends came to dissuade him, to try to persuade him not to enter into this pact with the powers that lie beyond the strength of Man. You are sick of anxiety and grief, they said. A man must live as long as he has life in him. He must go about his business, getting himself food and shelter.

When the death had been consummated and Joan had been taken away, they came again. Certain of his neighbors came to sit with him, to talk with him of every man's common sorrow.

"Helen Ware was a fine woman too," one said. "Two fine women he had. And grieved for the first from the bottom of his heart."

"Joan went the way Helen went."

He did not answer them.

"You've got here near two hundred acres. A man's land needs his care. As I came through the farther field and over the creek, horseback, I said to myself: 'Stoner Drake has been busy inside the house, sickness in family, that I well know. A fine field he's got here, but shows neglect, come up all in weeds, no cover crop sowed after the wheat.'"

"And trouble or not, when you go out of a morning, strong after you've slept . . ."

"Grief or not, you feel new-made . . ."

"How many sheep, on the average, does he keep? He's got a fine flock."

"About how many sheep, Stone, do you aim to run?"

"About a hundred and fifty," another answered, Drake being quiet. His daughter, Martha, stood behind her father's chair, or she brought a small jug of sweet cider. She was twenty years old, small and dark as her mother Helen had been. Her brothers, Arthur and Benjamin, both older than herself, were gone the way of Joan, each leaving a small child, John Thomas and Jocelle the names

4

of these. Having taken the cider quietly, the men spoke again:

"He's a strong man. How could he content himself indoors? There's hardly a man his equal in a field."

"In the harvest once he wore all the young men out. Not a one could keep his pace."

"Or the day the surveyors came. Stoner Drake worked all the young men down."

"I heard you had a bunch of cattle fit now to fatten. I'm in the market to buy some six or eight. . . . A surplus of feed, and I thought I'd fatten some cattle this fall." This man talked at length of the cattle, of the food ration he meant to try, of winter fattening. "I'd like to see any you've got to spare, Stone."

"I've got five ready to fatten," Drake said.

The men talked further of this matter, drawing it forth. They would go out and look at what Drake had, they said. They took up their hats and made ready to go outside, lingering. Drake called his black servant from the kitchen and told her to bring to him the stable man. "Take these gentlemen out, Nathan, and show them the young steers," he said.

The men lingered. "Come on with us, Stone," one said.

"I'll not unsay what I've said," he answered them. He spoke quietly, but his voice mounted in passion as he repeated what he had declared. "I know my fields. I plowed here when I was a boy. My father bought from his wife's

5

family, their home place, from the Ainsleys. They're mine, then, two ways. First in the talk of the Ainsleys—old Grannie Ainsley and my mother, Jocelle Ainsley, that died here in the west room. Known to me again because I helped my father pay out the debt, plowed when I was a boy. See't you know your fields as well as I know mine! Brought in the fine stock to raise good horses. Vacations from college I ran the two-horse mower over the hayfields and made a hand in the harvest. I know every field and know how far each goes, up and down, and what limestone is on the under side. God knows I know. But so help me God, I'll never set a foot on earth again. No man will persuade me. I'll stay here and if God so desires he can rot me of my whole flesh. He can put thistles in my mouth for food and he can sink my acres into the bottomless pits of weeds and hell."

THE HOUSE

Beginning at the hearthstone where Drake sat frequently in a stout hickory chair: The room about him was the diningroom of the house, used as a hall for general gathering. It measured twenty-four feet by twenty-six. At the north side stood the fireplace, the hearth of which was of smooth flags that lay slightly tilted to an uneven level now after many years of use, that reached three feet back from the chimney. Broad maple boards made the floor.

Two large brindled dogs of mixed breed sometimes lay not far from the fire, or later a rat-dog held the place, or a dark hound. Two uncurtained windows were in the west wall, and a door that opened to a small porch. A table for dining stood well back toward the south wall, but it was dragged to the middle of the floor when meals were served. At the left of the fireplace a tall cupboard with glass doors held several hunting weapons and a long fox-horn. At the right two doors entered, the one the kitchen through a pantry, and the other a small stairway that arose to a back room above.

Fourteen rooms, counting all, spread forward, above and beneath the great rock chimney. A door in the east wall of the diningroom opened into the main hall of the house and here a staircase reached to a hall above.

Drake walked up and down this staircase, the master of the house. His strong step was often heard beating the treads of the stairs. Above, he walked the length of the upper hall to a small door at the rear that gave onto a small balcony looking toward the barnlots and the fields. He wore slung about his shoulder a strap supporting a short hunting horn. Three short blasts on the horn would bring his chief man, an overseer, Foster, or Wright, or Tobin, whatever the name of the man thus employed. One blast would bring the stable hand; and two, the field laborer. Sometimes an old conch shell that hung in the upper hall would be used, or if the men were far, in fields beyond the

7

creek, the bell at the roof above the small balcony would be tapped, the bell-rope hanging near the door and well within the reach of a hand.

Back to the hearthstone, the journey to the upper window being done, the hickory chair would give forth minute creaking sounds as it pulsed with the pulsing life of the large man. If he tapped the floor with his heel, the kitchen woman would come to the door to the right of the chimney. An inquiry:

"Did Lem bring the mules back from the further pasture?"

"I don't know, sir. I don't know."

"Find out and tell me. Plain facts, I want. No lies."

The door that went toward the kitchen would flip-flop lightly when the Negress went swiftly out. The kitchen was a room of many cupboards. The cooking range stood to the side of the fireplace. On the open hearth a slow fire often smoldered, where irons were set in the embers, where bread was often set on the hearth to rise. The outer door opened into a passage that ran between the kitchen and a farther cabin which had been the first house. This passage, now open overhead and paved with flagstones, had once been the dog-run or the dog-alley, and this name lingered. Much of the labor of the kitchen occurred here in fine weather; here the dogs were fed.

In summer the birds would begin their early-morning jargoning soon after three o'clock, waking in the high trees

8

before the south wall, the last cry of the owl having rolled, flute-like, across the waning dark. With the singing of the birds would come the low thunder of the swallows as they left the east chimney and took to the air. For an hour or more the doves, the redbreasts, the cardinals, the thrushes, the jays, and the mockingbirds would pitch their singing among the trees, and off toward the south pasture among the overgrown shrubs of bridal-wreath and hackberry, the tinkle of the bellbird and the swift running cry and trill of the song-sparrow. Doors would be rattled within and a window thrown open, the hinge of the shutter singing roughly against the timbre of the birds. The barnyard animals at the rear of the house would begin a sudden flare of crying, a querulous and passionate greeting for the approach of their fodder. Then, within the house, a swift strong step would sound on the stairs.

The house had been built in portions, as the needs and the means of the owners had allowed. First had been built the cabin at the north end of the aggregate, and this building had been the first home of the Ainsleys on Wolf Lick Creek. Soon, across the passage or dog-run, another stout log structure had been built. When the house had been enlarged to the proportions of a country mansion, the second log house had been made a part of the final dwelling. Covered with weatherboards and raised to the full height of the main structure with rooms above, only the snug warmth of the rooms in winter and the sheltered

9

coolness in summer made a reminder that the kitchen and the diningroom were of the ancient log house.

JOAN

As an infant, Jocelle was taken by her mother to live in a small house in Anneville, the way there passing along sandy county roads and highroads, the turnings and shift-ings of rolling plain and hill scarcely remembered. In the town food came frequently from the distant farm, Wolf-lick—eggs, chickens, butter, bacon, and meal. Sometimes Jocelle, but not Catharine, went back along the highroad, over a bridge, into a turning sandy way between high woodlands, across then a lifting hill and into a gate where three beeches stood above a clump of wild-cherry hedge, to be again in the place where she was born.

"Call me Joan," her grandfather's wife said to her.

"Grandmother Joan?" Jocelle asked.

"I don't care," she replied, after a little thought. "Let it be Grandmother Joan if you like that."

Jocelle knew that her own name, Jocelle, had come to her from her grandfather's mother, and that the name had been Josephine Ellen. A Negro nursemaid, a slave-woman, had condensed the mellow vowels and brought the two names together into one word. It had thus become a family name, their own, and other Ainsleys had carried it thus

10

through life. In secret Jocelle sometimes called the handsome woman, her grandfather's bride, "Grannie Joan,"
or, following the science of the slave, "Grajoan."

This woman had been lately married to Jocelle's grandfather. She was strong, working about the kitchen yard,
directing the Negro helpers. Then her dark hair was
crinkled about her moist face and her dress would become
wet along the back between the shoulders. Her face was
ruddy and her breath deep. Stoner Drake would draw her
into his arms when he came into the house, thrusting
Jocelle aside once when she put herself between their
knees.

"One of the old hens left her nest," Joan said. "Left the
eggs to cool. Stayed off all night and a day."

"Those sour old fowls. Egad, I'll wring all their necks if
they vex Joan."

He took her away in the carriage to call at another farm.
Her fine cloth dress swept in ripples about her feet as she
walked out the door. There were sweet odors wherever
she was. She had forgotten Jocelle in walking out in her
fine bride-dress and in being lifted by her bridegroom into
the carriage. She was but thirty years old. Her eyes were
large and of a dark gray color, accepting happiness now,
and Jocelle was shamed by the veiled passion revealed in
the ascent to the carriage. But as Drake gathered up the
lines and drew them tight to set the horse off in a brisk

walk, she saw Jocelle cringing at the porch pillar as if she would shrink into it, and she waved her a good-by, calling: "Good-by, Jocelle, good-by."

Stoner Drake walked briskly about the farm, making ready, making plans, ordering his workmen. No hired laborer could match him in endurance. The coat of his fine stallion must be rubbed every day with a cloth or a brush. His trainer brought the two-year-olds to the long track that lay just beyond the fence and extended south from the paddock and the stables, and here they were worked out, either in harness or under a saddle. Drake would watch their going and he would call out: "Joan, Joan, come out and see the two-year-old mare in harness."

But there came a day when all the people of Wolflick were hurrying about, up and down stairs, getting things in the kitchen. Joan was sick in one of the upper chambers. It was morning, but all the work of the barns was stayed for Joan's sake. Jocelle had seen her arise from the couch below stairs where she had first lain and walk unassisted to the steps, but she saw her no more after she mounted the flight. Later Drake came from above and he waved the children out of his path, giving an order that they be taken to their homes. A buggy was quickly brought and the boys, J.T. and Walter, were taken away. Jocelle walked out, past the stables, turning about, feeling twisted and shriveled within, for J.T., her cousin, had told her that Joan would surely die. She stayed at the farm because nobody remembered to take her away. Nobody remembered to give her food, but she found something, and later she fell asleep on a divan in the parlor. When she awoke the gray of the dawn was faintly powdered through the room. Voices were speaking near. A strange woman's voice:

"She's gone, We can't help it."

A firm stride came down the hall and across the floor of the room. Stoner Drake was speaking, his voice high-pitched and scarcely recognized:

"If Joan dies I'll never, so help me God, set my foot on earth again. If Joan Drake dies, I'll never . . . I'll never. Hear me as I say it, my hand raised. It's past belief of the mind of man. If Joan dies I'll never set my foot on God's green earth again while time lasts. . . ."

On another day an elegant quiet lay through the house, strangers coming in and out on tiptoe. Joan's funeral went down the avenue, but Stoner Drake walked away to some upper back room, taking leave of it when it passed the portico. Jocelle did not go with the funeral. When the last carriage had rolled down the avenue, she went back through the empty house to the upper rear room where her grandfather stood looking from the window toward the fields. He thrust her from the room with a quick gesture and turned back toward the window. She was four and a half years old at that time, in 1901.

13

MARTHA

1903, and Martha going to the stable to get her horse
Dove, walking down the corridor of the farther building,
looking in stall after stall, calling "Dove," calling: "You,
Dove, there! Where's Dove?" Her feet dusted carelessly
in the dry beaten floor and her small whip beat a rhythm
on her skirt. She, thus, still young, twenty-five, and the
horse no longer Dove but Comet, her step light still but
more firm. Riding through the front avenue under the
sugar trees and over the fill where the water of the pond
lapped softly against the stones. Her eyes were dark and
bright. There was a catch in the flesh beneath the eyes, a
motion derived from long secrecy in love.

The stable was in three main parts, each part entered
by a wide doorway that fronted toward the south, the
whole structure being west and north of the dwelling. Of
the stable the middle section reached highest and was
adorned at the ridge with lightning rods, and when the
sun shone, the dull white of the walls and the glistening
gilt of the metal rods gave a glow that met the brilliant
glow on the coat of the great stallion. This animal, horse
or jack, whatever his name as the years passed, was kept
in a stall within the middle doorway, or was let run in a
pasture that reached farther toward the west. The mares
would graze in the front pasture, the long open stretch of

14

woodland that lay before the house and reached out to the highroad. Martha, in the stable door, calling "Dove," calling "Comet," would wait until a low whinny told her in what stall her horse would be, and her laughter would answer. She would lead her beast out then past the line of stalls, past the enclosed stall that held the blustering stallion.

Late at night, it being now 1913 or later, she would visit each hearth and there she would carefully rake together all the coals of fire and cover them over with a dry, deadened ash. The half-musical scraping of the shovel went as the last sound through the house, and it fell on the young, drowsing ears of Jocelle, of the young men, J.T. and Walter, as some useless and imperative ceremony. Walter had called this midnight visitation of the woman and the shovel the Curfew, and later the name was applied to the woman alone.

"Here comes Curfew." The words went through the still house as the light step came along the hall, the faint beating of the metal tools, the shovel and tongs throbbing together as she walked. Drowsy voices of the young men speaking:

"Suppose the house should catch fire."

"Never set his foot on earth in all God's any-more."

"It won't burn tonight, though."

"No, it won't burn . . ."

Jocelle, lying in her bed, drowsed under her blankets,

heard the soft ghost as it came to her fire. She was twenty years old now, the year being 1917. The woman, the Curfew, leaned over the bright coals and was lit by the red glow that shone as a dull fire on her face, that went, a dull glow, into the folds of her robe. Leaning thus toward the grate and thus illuminated, she had an incandescence that seemed to come from the glowing filaments of her haunted being. She turned her head away from the coals of fire and looked across the intervening space toward the bed where Jocelle lay. A steady impersonal look passed between the eyes at the hearthside and the other eyes that were half opened in sleep and glowing like two small, red, unshaded lamps. The shadows gave the mouth by the hearth a broad lateral line that was now fixed and still. The woman at the hearth was carved out of some illumined stone and she looked with steady searching gaze across at the other one.

There was no word spoken. Sixteen years lay between these two watchers. The eyes beyond the folds of the blanket were drowsed within and lit without with a firm shield of red light so that they told nothing. Jocelle now had a lover, and thus she had passed beyond the former relation of wondering child and young aunt about whom lay a mystery of unguessed experience. The statue beside the hearth, carved now in fire, did not yield its gaze, nor did the latitude of the carved mouth shrink or the lines quiver. It saw, in this moment of vision, underneath feeling and dutiful devotions, the lonely Will, the wish, the desire of the heart, housed within walls, blowing wild notes on a conch-horn.

At length the lids slowly drooped over the sleeping eyes, and the bright reflection there went back to the embers. Curfew then, not having extinguished this light, turned slowly about to the coals of natural fire which she carefully covered with the gray ash.

WOLFLICK

The land rolled in broad undulations of green if the season were moist, or of brown during the dry autumn months, and the landscape was not unlike the swell of an active sea, lifting in large billows or sinking into a trough. The roads rayed outward from the towns, going as the land went, rolling in constant curves around the hillsides or down into the creek valleys. There was sufficient soft limestone to make a firm roadbed, or near the creeks the roads were often made of gravel. Later, the coming of gasoline traffic brought changes in the methods of road-building. A few roads were broadened to become boulevards between the large towns. The inland counties then had but one or two good roads that were quickly whipped to dust by the motor vehicles, and the network of county roads became ill-tended lanes over which vehicles jolted as best they might. Thus Wolflick became year by year a more remote place, lying far, on a crossroad, scarcely vis-

17

ited except by those who had some urgent need to go there.

From the windows no other house was visible, but in the spring the fires of distant plantbeds, on other farms, rolled upward, at first red with flame and later as a smoldering fire that stood all day as a strange tree far against the sky. Within the barnyards Lem, the Negro man, and Chariet, his wife, cared for the sheep and the cows, or Chariet would set the hens and bring the new-hatched chickens to house them in the little hutches. Lem was a good hand with the sheep. He could gather them out of a field with his cries and bring them back to the stable for the night, never moving from the stable gate, and he would count them as they ran past his knees.

Jocelle was thirteen years old then. She would go with Chariet to the stable lot and she learned to draw milk from the cows, stooping under the animal's side. Her hand would be small and moist on the flesh of the beast, and the thin stream would run in spurts beneath her stroking palm. She felt then as if she were a part of the strong beast above her.

"Some men can't milk," Chariet said. "They hands are too big."

She would sit, looking upward, her eyes half closed, as if the milking were some part of her own nature, as if she felt a faint passion with it and lost herself in it, a half-smile on her drowsy brown face.

Jocelle milked the gentle big-faced cow that stood half

sleeping over her fodder. Lem would bring the cornstalks in armfuls and throw them before each beast, or he would walk away swiftly if the horn called him with one long blast.

At lambing time the sheep would be shut into the farther stable. The January cold; and sometimes the lambing would reach far into the night and the sheep would be crying. Lem would bring, now and then, a fainting lamb that seemed lifeless to the kitchen, and one of the women there would try to revive it before the hearth. Often it would revive, but sometimes, being chilled too much, it would not breathe again. These fainting lambs were called "dead lambs."

On a dull morning, cold outside rattling sleet against the windows, Lem brought a dead lamb to the kitchen and, laying it quickly on the floor near the hearth, he hurried away to the sheep. A lamp burned through the dark morning and lit the kitchen with a brown glow. Jocelle found the dead lamb soon after it was brought to the kitchen, for Chariet called her softly from the pantry door. It lay on its side, limp and cold, its little dark feet crumpled together. It had been the third of a litter and had been rejected by the mother.

Jocelle could not discover a throb of heart-beat under the soft, new-born wool. She laid the dead lamb on a piece of old blanket before the fire and, pulling Chariet's shawl over her head, she ran to the stable to ask Lem to milk a little milk from one of the ewes. She had several times helped Chariet revive a dead lamb. She brought the milk in a little white teacup and set it near the fire to keep warm.

"Law, it might not live," Chariet said. "Weak before it got borned and little chance it's got."

"And what for is life to it?" Chariet's mother, the old woman in the corner beyond the lamplight, half hidden in the shadow of the stove, asked again: "What's life to it?"

Jocelle went to the diningroom and she asked Drake to give her a teaspoonful of whisky from the little jug in the gun cabinet. "To bring back a dead lamb," she said. She mixed the whisky with two spoonfuls of the milk. Then, with Chariet to help, she held the lamb's mouth open and poured the fluid slowly down the little throat. The little tongue was cold and still. She rubbed gently on the throat to help the flow of the small stream downward, and she held the lamb near the fire, waiting to discover if the heart would beat, if there still might be some small throb in the lamb's breast.

"Won't bleat e'er baa. And if it lives, no eow will ever take it. Have to raise it on a bottle."

Chariet did not reply to the old woman, and Jocelle continued to warm the lamb at the fire. If it lived, Chariet would give it milk from a bottle for a few weeks and later it would run with the other lambs in the spring pasture. Jocelle knelt near the fire now, holding the lamb, and

presently she saw a flicker of life in the tongue and felt a
faint breath on her hand. Then the lamb cried out a faint
bleat and the women laughed. Jocelle gave it a little more
of the milk and laid it within the blanket near the fire to
rest.

STONER DRAKE

Jocelle, a child eight years old, lately come back to live
at Wolflick, walked past her grandfather's chair in terror
while he sat brooding, being thankful if she was forgotten.
She would go with Martha to look for the lost turkey's
nest and she would call the fowl at the edge of the wheat-
field. Martha was light and quick, her step skipping
through the wheat. She sometimes went away to some distant place to study. She taught Jocelle to ride the small
brood mare. Both mounted, they rode up and down the
training track straight along the fence and southward before the stables. There would be laughter and outcry.
Martha's voice twitted, more firm than the voice of the
swallows that went swiftly about the eaves of the white
buildings. "Get Jocelle the little whip. Hi! Lem, there,
bring Jocelle the little blue crop."

One day Jocelle found herself alone with her grandfather, and the stillness of the room told her that he was
looking at her. Outside rain fell and the morning was
chilly. The world seemed suddenly to have become very

21

still. No beasts were crying at the barns and no birds were calling above the eaves. She looked up suddenly and she thought that she would run away through the rain to the old buggy house across the paddock and find something she had hidden there. Her grandfather smiled at her, and his smile, coming full upon her, meant for her, delayed her terror, so that she found herself standing between his knees looking up into his ruddy face. What did she think about? he asked, speaking softly. What did she think? and what did she like best? He looked at her in amused disbelief, as if he scarcely could believe that she could think of anything at all. His strong thin lips bent and curved about his words. His large body leaned forward toward her. He kissed her forehead. His hands brushed lightly along her small arms.

She did not think of anything, she told him, shy before him, looking down, smiling, her soft cheek against his rough face. He pushed her gently off so that he might look at her, his hands moving in convulsive tenderness on her thin shoulders. What, he asked her, did she think about yesterday?

"I thought about Geography."

"Oh, ho! Geography. And what is that?"

"In my book. It teaches about the earth on which we live."

"What is a river, then?"

"A body of water that flows through the land."

22

"Sakes bless us! She does know. And what else?"

"I can name all the oceans."

"And the continents? What is an island?"

"Is a small body of land surrounded by water."

"What is the shape of the earth?"

"It's round like a ball. It turns every day on the axis."

"What's the color of the earth?"

She did not know. She tried to think of a name for the colors blended in the fields. The question was not in the book.

"Once I saw the earth, the whole earth. Night of the eclipse it was up against the moon," she said.

"And how did it look, child?"

"Oh, it was *black*. The blackest thing ever I did see."

"Black. It was black. . . . The blackest thing in the heavens. . . . The blackest thing she ever did see. Black. This earth. Our earth, on which we live. . . . Black. She saw it was black."

"Cities and towns, capitals of countries, seaports. Things people do. In the book, and the teacher showed us how it is with some pictures. Pretty houses, one in Italy and one, I remember, in some other place, I don't remember where. Palaces and libraries and town halls and churches." She made an upward motion with her hand, building a shape in the air, supplying what she could not remember.

"Then I made up a place," she said.

"What place?"

"I made it. Bridges over a river. A tower and a palace. Beautiful. . . . Places to go. Long roads with marble walls and gates made out of curly iron bars. The houses all made out of fine marble, some canary yellow and some blue."

A curious fantasy, he said. She made a Place. He repeated what she said and she told further. It was thus there, and thus. All the shapes there were splendid. She made them with her lifted hands. She could not tell all of it with words, but she made him see the Place she had made, telling with her short crippled phrases and the hints from pictures, from the telling of the schoolmistress. There would be a river bank carpeted with flowing grass that would bend in a light wind, the whole grass flowing with the turning of the hills. The water would be clear and clean and it would ripple in the sun. Thus, she said, it would be, and thus.

"What fantasy is this? A Place she made. Towers and palaces. I'll give you a waterfall to go in your Place."

"I know! I forgot it. The water of a river falls over a great high rocky wall."

"The water sparkles in the sunlight. Spreads like a sheet of silver over stone. A white tower, she says. A long marble stair goes up to the top where you can look out. You'd see the whole of the Place. Gates of smooth wrought-iron. Fine houses along the way, some little and some great, marble fretwork and pillars. Colonnades. Porticoes. Down the

24

river is a dock where the ships come to land. Stairs go down to the water, broad steps out of granite, any color you say. The sails are made of blue or red or yellow."

"And, yes," she said. She was out of breath with delight.

"Along the wharf is a marble parapet, a low wall you can look over to see the ships come to dock."

"All the people sing together."

"In a wide square. The floor is paved with colored stones in blocks of blue or red or purple. Whichever you like best."

"Have it blue, with a little red."

"Back across the beautiful street is a woodland. Tall shapely trees and green verdure. Down the river are spires and cupolas and towers, out of fine fretted stone, as far as ever eye can see."

In a trance she answered him, saying more than she knew, words coming to her lips beyond memory. "Because God is there."

"God spreads through the whole place."

"As far as ever you can see."

He began to speak, looking past her, catching tight to her shoulders:

" 'Thine hands have made me and fashioned me together round about; yet thou dost destroy me. Remember, I beseech thee, that thou hast made me as the clay; and wilt thou bring me into dust again?' "

She tried to look past his staring eyes and to draw her-

25

self from his clutching hands. "A waterfall. Bridges over a river. Sails, blue, on the ships." She murmured, trying to bring back the Place they had built together. Frightened, she began to cry out softly, panting in terror.

" 'Thou hast clothed me with skin and flesh, and hast fenced me with bones and sinews. . . . Fashioned me together round about . . . made me as the clay; and wilt thou bring me into dust again . . . ?' "

These strange words were formed to pass with the bending and twisting of his hard mouth. Suddenly his face withdrew upward and she was thrust away, pushed backward by his strong stiffened arms, but she did not fall. "Away with you. There's no such. There's no such city. Go on with your lies. Go on. Pattern got by men. Out of his befuddled life. What's he? On one side he's a pulen, unknowen brat. On the other he's a senile, slobberen, totteren, forgetten old man. Who wants to be such a crawlen thing? A new-born, unborn, who wants to be, a unknowen fœtus, a snake, a lizard, a blob of greasy slime, proto, proto, proto? What's a city but a hog-wallow of noise and sellen filth? . . . Go on away. Out of my sight."

II

Not far from the house where Jocelle and her mother lived, in Anneville, a building was being constructed. Piles of lumber were brought to the open spaces about the proposed house and men there were sawing beams or planing surfaces. There was a sharp musical note to cry out over the street when the mason struck a brick with his trowel building foundation or chimney.

With two other children, Jocelle, being seven years old, would play among the piles of lumber, or, when the finishing woodwork was being prepared, she would sit among the fresh shavings, adorned with wooden curls. She would hear the oaths of a carpenter when he damned a blunt tool or sent forth blasts of profane distress when a beam fell through his grasp. As she gathered long curls of shavings and fastened them to her hair, she would hear the whisperings about her ears, the sibilance of finely cut wood, and she would feel herself to be as the angels in heaven, having curls enough, being made lovely and good as far as the mind could imagine.

Among the workmen there was a tall strong man, a man of no discernible age, independent of age. He had strong arms and legs that stiffened under great loads and bent to strut away, carrying the heaviest beams with the Negro helpers. His name was Dickon. As he worked with his plane or his saw, he would suck at large quids of tobacco and often he would spit a great mouthful of brown liquid into the sawdust or the shavings. It was whispered about that Dickon had written a book. Few had seen the book, but there were vague reports of it. For this report he was looked upon with distrust mingled with amusement that veered toward pity. For a book, written by one who was seen daily, who ate food as did other men, who hauled burdens with his hands and whose feet stepped over the stones of the pavings as did those of the least, was distrusted; as if old Sol Dickon had contrived to get, somehow, a grip upon the throats of his townsmen.

Standing to watch the progress of the house, Jocelle heard certain voices above the whispers of her curls. Three men had met beside the saw-bench while Dickon walked stiffly out of the improvised doorway.

"He's written a book," one said.

"It's got not one comma nor period from cover to cover," another.

"Have you ever seen it?"

"Not I. And what's more, I never saw man that had."

"I saw a man had read a part of it." The words mum-

28

bled as if danger threatened. "He made no mention of how the commas were, but he said it's got not one grain of sense inside or out."

The speakers were gone and the work went forward, Jocelle continually supplied with crisp curls. A great blast from Dickon's quid splattered into the fallen shavings, and Jocelle caught at her parings and ran swiftly back to miss the flow. She left the lumber completely until she should forget what had happened there. Then Dickon flung out a blast of hard, sharp words to follow, and Jocelle knew that the tobacco had been sent forth as a first volley to drive the children away. There were oaths in his speech. His words seemed to burst from his roughly shaven face and his stiff throat as if they were pinned together with threats that would crack the day into splinters and rip apart the earth itself.

When he had spoken thus in anger, Jocelle ran to the farther end of the lot of ground and waited. Standing there with another child, Rose, she saw Dickon walk toward the house with a door-frame above his shoulders. Rose tried to persuade her to ask him as he passed: "Did you write a book, Mr. Dickon?" but she would not ask this.

The boys of the town called Dickon "King Solomon" or "Sol" because he had no wife, and the name had become fixed upon him. It was said that he was trying to build an airship. He had rented an old house at the edge of the town, and there, shut carefully within, he had worked for years at some secret labor. A light often burned in the house until late in the night. Once three boys tried to persuade Jocelle to shout to him: "How's your airship, Mr. Dickon?" but she would not. The house was closed behind stout shutters and the yard was grown with tall grass through which a path went in a straight line to the door.

Dickon lodged at a house in the town, not far from the place where Jocelle lived. The child Rose was the daughter of this house, and she would often call Jocelle to her gate or take her within to play on the stair or run through the upper passages. Sometimes their game took them to Mr. Dickon's room at the front of the house above stairs. At the threshold the carpet came to an end, and, within, the bare floor stretched evenly away, unbroken by rug or mat. The bed was set in a far corner, exact and plain, set squarely beside the wall. There were two chairs, but no dresser or wardrobe. A pail of water stood on a window sill, a pan for washing near it. On a table lay three books and a few blank sheets of paper. An oil lamp stood above the paper, stiff and smooth and clear. Rose was obliged to clean the lamp chimney each day, to rub it until it shone brightly. There was nothing more in the room. Three books, blank sheets of paper, a bright light prepared, the washpan, the pail, the bed, and the chairs; these were all.

"I wouldn't dare leave a crumb of dirt on the lamp," Rose whispered.

The child tended the lamp, listening for any step that might come on the stairs, and went quickly away. She made Jocelle promise never to tell anyone that she had passed the threshold.

One day while Jocelle played among the shavings of wood, a small girl named Celia passed along the street. The child laughed softly to see what a wealth of material for play lay about their feet, but presently she drew Jocelle aside and whispered fearfully that Mr. Dickon did not believe in anything.

"How can you prove it?" Jocelle asked.

"Everybody knows it. He does not even believe in heaven and hell."

Jocelle was afraid with Celia's fear. "Nor in love," Celia said.

"What kind of love?"

"You know. Love. Like they read about in novels."

Plain unbelief settled about the remembered spareness of the room, about the clear lamp and the few sheets of unwritten paper. Dickon walked heavily through the emptiness he had devised.

"He wrote it into a book," Celia said.

"How do you know?"

31

"I heard it said so."

The man Dickon went past them as they stood huddled together to whisper. He was drawing his long thumb across the surface of a planing knife, shouting back toward the house: "Gosh all Jupiter! Bring here the oil can."

"And what else?" Jocelle asked.

"And wrote he didn't believe in the Holy Ghost."

"He'll be struck dead some day by lightning."

Jocelle spoke this last. It was a belief that passed about among the children. She had never uttered it before, but, having heard it, the judgment came easily from her as being the conclusion toward which Celia's horror moved.

Celia walked away down the street, making a mouth that signified complete shock and condemnation, her upper teeth biting her lower lip and drawing it inward. She looked back from time to time to make sure that her condemnation would be felt anew, and each time the grimace was enacted. Dickon's long arms would be reaching, drawing boards here and there, as if he drew things through the town, as if he reached through the streets and houses to take whatever his rough gray face demanded. Jocelle disregarded all beliefs and threats, and, since her curls were stale, she crept close to the work-bench and caught the bright parings of poplar wood to make herself a new loveliness.

If Dickon were unaware of others as near, he would often be speaking, muttering words or comments upon his learning. Speaking: "Symbolic diagram . . . system of mathematical or chemical connection . . . Or a copy multiply. Multiply with this. Gelatine copying apparatus. . . . Hah, hah, hah. . . . Autograph, chirograph, holograph, lithograph, photograph . . . seismograph, telegraph. . . . Graph, Greek, *graphos,* written, writing. I write. I write about. . . . Grapher, one versed in graphy. . . . Graphical, vividly descriptive. That is to say, very graphic. Verigraphic. . . . Hah, hah, hah. Lifelike. Graphology, then. Inferring character from handwriting. Graphy, and that's the most useful of all the graphs, root hog or die. Here you've got *geo.* . . . Any schoolboy . . . Biblio plus graphy, biblio-graphy, for the colleges. Graphite, plumbago . . . Greek, *grapho* again. I write with plumbago, is what it comes to. Say yesterday you walked down toward Sycamore Valley and say you happened on a man was a thief. Shy, he was, sidled over against a fence, all the time his sack full of hens he'd plucked offen Squire Bailey's roost. . . . I write with plumbago. . . . 'Hit's fine weather,' he says. Thieven makes a man shy. 'You lost, I reckon, all your pullets in the flood last week,' I says. 'Every damn pullet I had,' he says. 'Get a fresh start,' I says. 'Here's where I go in,' he says, and he goes, shy, in Trotter's gate. A hungry snake, I reckon, inside his rennet. . . . Rennet, the inner mucous membrane of the fourth stomach of a calf or other young ruminant. Written runnet. Rennet written runnet. Hah, hah, hah. His soul damned with thievery but nobody cared, and the least of all them that damned 'im. All I cared was would he leave my things, chickens or what-not, alone. . . ."

One day Jocelle's mother looked at her growing frame and said that her dress had become too small. The gaze that accompanied this searching speech entered the scanty garment and measured there the slowly lengthening limbs and the broadening form of the seven-year-old child. Then Jocelle hated her increased frame and she would look down with shame upon her hands and legs that seemed coarse and large. She would try to draw her thin knees under her dress when she sat down. Her mother's large, shapely form stood high above her or bent suddenly to sit in a chair. A conviction had been settled upon her; she must not outgrow her clothes. Her life in the town seemed temporary then, a season of unwanted growth, and this illusion of impermanence was strengthened by the knowledge that her mother did not own the house in which she lived. Her mother owed rent for the house. The knowledge of rent which was now and then unpaid for several paying days, weighing heavily upon her, forbade her to grow, but suddenly, from time to time, she would know that more growth had come to her.

34

A voice speaking in anger above her head: "I can't take you with me, and I can't go to Wolflick to live. What's then to do?"

Catharine was large and florid and hearty. "You're just another Drake," she said to Jocelle one day in vexation. Her eyes were large and bold, but her gaze was often misty and she seemed then to dream. Her hair was almost black. It grew straight from her forehead and was rolled and waved above her ears into large sleek pillars that melted into the tightly looped masses at the back of her head.

Jocelle would sometimes lean against her mother's shoulder when she sat in a chair, but she was always pushed away. She could not remember that she had ever sat in her mother's lap or been held in arms. She was proud of her mother's fine dresses. She would run up the small stairway to get a comb or to fetch slippers or garters, or she would run to the end of Hill Street to find a Negro woman to wash Catharine's linen. "Run on," Catharine would say, her gaze sullen and misty as she thrust Jocelle from the house door. A man came to sit with her in the small parlor. He was a stranger to the town who came there from time to time to sell something. The intercourse in the parlor mounted at each visit from badinage to ardor, and the presence of this strange man in the house made Jocelle remember her father who had been dead three years. Once the strange man, Mr. Farris, asked her to give him a kiss, but Jocelle, remembering Ben Drake, slapped at the mouth that was thrust near. The house would be full of hurried preparations, with fruit and banter, while Farris was in the town or while he sat within. When he was gone, Catharine was sullen and angry until some message told of his next coming.

Jocelle moved in and out of the fog of this excitement. Farris was hateful to her. She knew that he was afraid of her, that he drew back from her as if he thought she might spit upon him. His face was clean-shaven and his clothes were fine. He would brush upward on his frizzly hair and set the curl backward from his brow. His eyes were clear and his face was ruddy. Jocelle would not play with any toy he gave her until she had subtracted it from the giver, until she had made a convincing pretense that it had come from some other.

"Who gave you the blue ball?" Catharine would ask, wanting to hear a name.

"Rose gave it to me."

"She did not. Fred Farris gave it."

"Rose."

Outside the small house the town reached, right and left, house after house along the quiet streets. Wolflick was never visited now. Now and then a laborer from that place would stop in a cart before the house in Anneville and leave a gift of provender—fruits of the season or meal or poultry. He would bring no messages and presently he would be gone. Jocelle wished her house to be as the other houses appeared, up and down the street, quiet and undistinguished.

"If you won't say Frederick gave you the red hoop, he'll never give you anything else," Catharine said to her.

"He never did give me any."

She had the hoop taken from her and broken into pieces that were thrust into the kitchen fire.

She played in the small garden behind the place where she lived, making play under a little quince tree. The town seemed to rest under a mid-summer quiet. The people went and came about their accustomed pleasures or necessities. They walked past in the street or they went inside their doors; they bought food at the grocery shops or they called to one another as they passed, seeming to say little. They were not afraid of one another, nor did they give gifts so far as she knew. A faint haze of things known and unknown spread around her. Those things which she could never bring together into a pattern of thought were left unrelated, floating in a fog. She was not often unhappy. There seemed to be nothing outside her door like to that which resided within, but Celia would come to play with her. Sometimes she would go with Catharine to the church, or go with her to call at one of the houses up the street.

In autumn Jocelle went each day to a school where she had learned to read the year before. With the other children at playtime she learned to catch a small ball while her fingers snatched at little iron pegs that were called jacks. Her skill in this game mounted, and it was her delight to excel her companions. The days ran as a merry mechanism that whirred with her increasing agility with the ball, so that her feet seemed scarcely to be touching the ground as her multiplication tables were learned and her mind bounced lightly among the things of the readers and the small geography book. If her lessons were neglected for a day, the quality of the ball played over her unknowing so that she tossed easily and heedlessly upon this ignorance and bounced lightly to the foot of the class to mount later to her place near the head.

At home, impelled by the ball, coming in rhythmic clatter down the small corner stairs, she would see the room below laid out in a distorted design that was laterally over-broad and flattened against the floor. It was early winter. Coming thus one day from above she saw the sheet of paper on which Catharine was writing, and she read the bold letters, "Dearest Frederick, my husband."

The following day Catharine said to her: "Make the house clean. Call the maid. Tell her . . ." She would be hurrying above, finding things out of trunks. She would be curling her hair before the mirror or standing to try on a gown while a dressmaker pinned tight the seams. The

one looked for, Mr. Farris, came. They, these two, were
in the small parlor among the upturned boxes and they
were laughing continually together. Jocelle ran away to
school and there a girl, Celia, told her that her mother
was going to marry that day. Telling of the wedding the
child caught her lower lip with her teeth and held it, the
grimace of the shocked gossip.

"Yesterday he got a divorce from Mrs. Farris," Celia
said.

Jocelle pretended to know something of this, wanting
to shield her mother from the bitten lip. In the afternoon
she left the geography class and ran swiftly out at the
schoolhouse door. No one called her back. At her home
Catharine was dressed in a fine dress of blue cloth. She
told Jocelle to put on her best dress and to be quick.
"Where have you been gone all day?" she asked in vexation.

"What one is my best?" Jocelle asked.

Catharine was angry at this question, approaching tears.
"Your . . . haven't you got a brown dress with a sash?"

There had been one the winter before, but it was now
worn out and outgrown. "What have you got then?" The
question was flung in indifferent anger from the face that
was bent near to the mirror to arrange a curl. Jocelle had
only the dress she had worn to the school. Viewed now,
beside the blue gown, her shoes and stockings were in bad
order. Catharine bit her lips and became deeply flushed,

but she did not speak at once. She began to put on her hat before the glass. The house was cold and disordered. Catharine walked here and there, but finally she went to the door and called a man who was passing. An order was swiftly given and almost at once a driver came from the livery stable with a conveyance. He must take the child and her baggage to Wolflick farm.

"Put on your coat and hat and be quick," Catharine said. "And take whatever you want with you."

Jocelle turned about swiftly to obey, the tears of surprise and confused emotions rushing to her eyes. She could scarcely gather her few clothes together. Her schoolbooks and a few toys were gathered with her clothing into a basket. "Must I take my silver cup?" she asked, and the reply: "I don't care what you take, so you hurry." She was to be eight years old in three days more and, while she packed the things into the basket, she remembered this, subtracting from the date any significance it might ever have held for her. She was glad to be going to Wolflick, for she would see Martha, her aunt, there. But she was shamed to be thrust there thus and confused to try to know why she was sorry to go or why glad, and thus her tears engulfed her, her mother calling: "Hurry! She always was as slow as a snail." Jocelle feared the upturned house, but she dared not ask where Catharine would be going or where she would go after Wolflick, or what dress she would wear tomorrow, or what would become of her life at the school or her passage through the street. Her memory was drowned in impermanence and fear. Remembering some trinkets and bits of clothing that she prized, put above stairs in a drawer of an old chest, she yielded completely to the refrain that beat in distress over her, the passionately breathed "Hurry" or "Hurry, Jocelle!" that fell from her mother's shortened breathing. She did not go upstairs to get the things there. She pulled her hood forward over her disordered hair and struggled swiftly with the sleeves of her coat.

Catharine took the basket and went with it to the pavement before the house, giving it to the driver who thrust it into the rear of the carriage. Jocelle climbed into the vehicle, her mother gently thrusting her from behind. "To Wolflick," her mother said to the driver, and remembered then that she had not kissed the child. She leaned nearer for one moment, without hurry; in one leisured and conventional instant, taking the child's hand, she said good-by and began some sentence of promise and explanation, but dropped the utterance unfinished, a sob in her breath, and the horse drew the carriage slowly away.

This, departure and advent, was long remembered. It was merged with a fog that lay among the distant winter-reddened hedges and with the feet of the horse that slopped through sandy quags. The woman receded as a blue

41

breadth of cloth going into a doorway among closing shadows, a restlessness bogged in passion and clothed richly in a temporary envelope of soft blue cashmere cloth made in the style worn in the parlors and churches at that season. The way was long, for the driver did not speak on the journey which required near three hours.

Martha, the daughter of Stoner Drake, was sitting at her desk in an upper room at Wolflick. She was slight, preoccupied with friends, memories, studies—all made in a university life that had been interrupted by the death of Joan. She sat over her desk in the twilight of a winter day. Her father's step came briskly up the stair and went down the long hall to the rear of the house, and later a tramping of feet on the flagstones. The loud-spoken interchanges with Wright, the trainer and overseer:

"Here, you, Wright, did you try out the mule colt in harness?"

"Drat Lem for a fool. Tell him I say fetch the mule colt here. I'll see for myself."

Shouted replies without meaning, and then: "What d'y'mean, Lem, to furnish out the mule with a collar to bind his neck and rub a sore? Here, take the colt to the stable and rub lard on the hurt. Call Chariet here. Did you, Wright, measure the oats? Make a measure of how much is left in the big bin. . . ."

The voices outside floated farther away or burst nearer, but the voice at the upper rear balcony remained constantly in admonition, or in broken soliloquy. "Drat all kingdom, but I've got a loggerheaded set." A run of swift notes on the calling horn and a Negro's gobbled words replied running above the crying of the calves and the shrieking of the swine. A low crunching of wheels on the wet driveway entered into the blended sounds, and later a soft, slow step on the stair. The door opened and Jocelle stood at the threshold looking within. She was white and cold, her face drawn and troubled. Martha laid down her papers wearily, annoyed by the interruption, and Jocelle, seeing Martha coming toward her, began to weep, hearing the great noise at the rear.

"Y'ought to have chosen a better day to come," Martha said. "And look, she's cold through and through. What, Honey, made you come such a boggy day as this?"

Jocelle was unable to tell her aunt that she had come there to live, that she had not chosen the day. Martha bade her dry her eyes. "The next time you must choose a bright warm day." Soft words made a temporary matter of the disaster. There would be something good for supper, head cheese and hot gritty mush with cream. The thought of the hot food heartened Jocelle and made her smile with Martha, and after that it was easy to say what pressed upon her tongue, to utter the two hard facts that would make Martha's speech swift and angry for a moment.

"Why didn't she tell us?" Martha asked. "But she's afraid, Catharine is. She's afraid of us." Accusing words

43

blamed Catharine, and Jocelle cried again. "To dump you out into the cold!" Martha said. She called Lem from the window, crying: "Bring more coal. Come to help here." Jocelle would sleep that night on a couch in Martha's room, and after that a room would be prepared for her. "Wants to be free of it, free of us, Catharine does," Martha said. She spread quilts before the fire to warm them and made Jocelle's bed. The hard part would be to tell Drake, she said. "He'll roar Catharine half off the earth, and roar me a part of the way, and you with me."

Jocelle was afraid of the long stable front and of the animals behind it. Wanting the warmth of a fire, Martha being gone, she played with her little ball far back in the diningroom. Drake seemed unaware of her. But one day he drew her to him, and the question, what did she think about? She thought about geography, about the world, the earth. Later she ran away in the cold to cry, sheltered by the stable wall, and crept back again to her play.

She knew Wolflick well, remembered from the time of her visits there in the lifetime of Joan, and she knew that she had been born there in the room behind the parlor, a room that Stoner Drake now used. She would look in at the door of this room, at the tall bed, the high chest over which hung a small mirror, the tall bureau, the washstand where water always stood ready for her grandfather's

44

bathing. The carpet would be dim with a gray ashy dust from the tobacco, but later Mrs. Wright would sweep it over and then dim flowers would appear in the black surface. A desk there was piled with papers, the kinds held down by paperweights. She was afraid of her fear of the room, fearful that it might increase, that she might overstep caution and handle the paperweights, but she would run frequently to the door when she knew that Drake was at the upper back window, and she would stretch her neck to see within without stepping over the door sill. She learned to be near the table when the meals were served that she might not be forgotten then. Asceticism lay about her without the cooling draft of prayers.

There were three small mulatto children in one of the cabins back in the farm, and these would toss and catch the little jack-ball with her on the floor of the west porch. Or she would take a bit of bread and meat in her pocket and go with the dark children to the stream far back among the fields to play there half the day. She would slip into the house and up to her bed after nightfall, her presence unmissed and her coming unnoticed. But sometimes an unexpected rain of questions would greet her:

"Where've you been all day?

"How'd you tear your dress half off?"

She would lie to save herself from blame or to enhance her importance, to make her presence somehow notable. She had torn her dress climbing the high fence to bring

45

the old turkey hen back from the farther grain field, she would say, a fiction, for the dress had met disaster on the top of the calf shed. Or she brought in fifteen eggs, filched from Mrs. Wright's basket, and pretended she had found them in a stray nest. In the glamour of the eggs she assumed importance at a supper table. Her lies made a fiction about Catharine from whom she had heard but once. A question set the myth astir:

"Here, you, Jocelle. When did you hear from Catharine, your mother?"

"I heard a little while back."

"Where is she now?"

"She's in Evansville."

She hid a letter from the mailbox out at the road-gate under a stone beside the pond in the front pasture. The geese came and pecked at the stone, but she left it hidden there and conceived that it had come from Catharine. When her grandfather complained of an unanswered letter and watched closely all the mail that was brought, she left the hidden piece lie, still pretending it was her own.

Her grandfather's step did not hush her laughter. The fine lines about his mouth seemed ready to break with grief or mirth. His hands were supple and strong and they were ruddy in the summer season when he worked on the upper front portico mending a harness or a tool. In winter he would sometimes mend a shoe for one of his hands, taking a last from the underpart of the kitchen

closet and pounding at the sole before the diningroom fire.
His fingers were ready to crumple into a fist leaving the
index finger free to point, so that, since this gesture came
frequently to his hands, Jocelle thought of it as being
the man himself, as if his whole body and being focused
to a sharp pointing finger. Around him lay the farm,
wound in enormous circles by the surrounding hills and
the focus of life that gathered to the barns and breeding
pens and drew them more inwardly toward the house,
the man there, the step on the stair, the sounding horn
at his tight lips, the pointing finger protruding from a
strong fist. She slipped out of the vortex on nimble feet.
She had a multitude of little things, claiming the snail-
tracks about the cellar door and the sow-bugs that ran
among the flagstones, the brilliant color in the wood-rot
of an old tree.

Her cousin, John Thomas Drake, whom she called J.T.,
came to spend the summer months at Wolflick. He was
the son of Arthur Drake who had been the first-born of
Stoner Drake and Helen Ware, and thus he was nephew
to Martha. Jocelle liked the time when he was at hand.
He was two years older than herself and something like
her in coloring, being half blond; but growing taller, his
face became long and thin, and he became a tall boy all
in one summer, laughing down upon her from the roof
of the barn, his long teeth glistening. He was careful. He
contrived a steel trap on the top of a high pole to catch

47

the hawks that were preying upon the barnyard fowls. He would shout to old Drake from the roof of the stable when he had found the leak in the roofing. Another cousin, Walter Drake, would come from time to time while J.T. was at hand. This one was a nephew to Stoner Drake and was thus a first-degree cousin to Martha, a few years older than J.T. The boys would borrow the guns from the cabinet and hunt squirrels in the creek tangles, but Walter cared little for the work of the farm.

The boys were something to themselves, bound together, racing away across the large pasture on the horses, called back and forbidden, wanting her to slip them the guns out of the house. Caught in a misdeed, she would snap the elastic of her garter for comment if no lie gave help to her, departing thus from a dangerous interchange with the man of the conch-horn. Gliding into her seat at the table, she would eat well of the foods there. Withdrawing herself by the gesture of her half-shrinking shoulders, she would clothe herself in affected inattention, or she learned to match inquiry into her affairs with childish ignorance or half-impudent titterings.

In winter the rooms beyond the two or three fires spread dark and cold. Often then she had an illusion of some presence or shape that followed her, so that she would run swiftly through a door after it was opened and clap the door shut to expel the coming form, whether it was conceived as having life or as ominously inactive. When Sol

Dickon came to the farm to work as carpenter for her grandfather, she thought that he, as a large shape on a stairway, had followed her there. She found a grotesque stone among some broken flags that were piled in a corner of the cowpen, a stone that resembled Dickon as his shape or quality had form in her mind. He was near at hand now, at the table for meals, walking about the back door, measuring with a line or a ruler. She rolled the horned-stone to a spot before the cow-stable door, and when the cows dropped their little upon it, she was content.

Drake, at this time, devised to build an open passage or bridge from the rear of the upper hallway to extend across the open space below and reach the roof of the cabin. Here, on this roof, he would build an outlook, partly enclosed overhead, from which he might view the whole reach of the barnyards and the near-lying fields. The structures were to be neatly built of wood. Sol Dickon was brought from the town to construct this platform and bridge, and while the work went forward, Dickon stayed at Wolflick. All day he hoisted timbers briskly and worked with his hammer and saw, and at night he slept in the room above the kitchen, the room reached by the corner stairway in the diningroom. At work he would talk frequently to himself.

49

"Help, I will, all I'm able. Won't set foot beyond house, s'elp 'im God, and so he anlarges his stride. . . . Then came Earth, Terra. Oceanos was born to Terra. That's the river that flows around the dry land. Won't set foot on earth while time lasts. . . ."

Drake at the upper window, looking out on the work, would ask a question. A broad gesture and a clear order would indicate his wish. "What, here, does this bridge rest on? How will it look pitched up here in the air?"

"On the house and the cabin, sir. No crazy scaffold-work about to fall down into your dog-run. A bridge to stay in place when I'm through. False-work, Mr. Drake. Down it comes when I'm through."

"Let it be a bridge, then. Arched, I said."

"As good a bridge as stands over any stream in the county. White timber, cut square and true, and arched underneath. Thrust out from wall to wall, fitten to touch your fine old house."

Drake went away from the upper window. He would send an order to town for the nails and bolts that were wanted. A prolonged, mirthless laugh followed his going. "Hah, hah, hah!"

A slow, improvised laughter, the mirth gone out of it, commented further on the departure. "Hah, hah, hah! Anger, gusts of busted strength. The earth rolls over, turns upside down and back between one day and the next. Old Drake blows a gust on a foxhorn ho-Wright-come-

Lem-you-here-you-black-jackass. Bring out the yearlen colts. Builds himself a bridge to walk over on and the Red Sea can go swish-floppety. After the bridge comes his lookout hoisted over the cabin, all on one level, y'understand. Never-say-die carved on his bones. . . . A good farm. Good stock, bred right. Builds himself here a longer dog-walk, a tight vow, a stronger s'elp me God to thrust the man a little further out over nature. . . . In beginning was Chaos, unformed matter. Runs then a long tale, natural processes. In the end Chaos. All wore out. Little monkey-shines done. Old man of the sea stays last. . . . Twenty-five pounds of eight-penny nails. . . ."

In the evening, after supper, the table being cleared from the middle of the floor, Drake pointed Dickon to a seat by the fire. A little rat-dog moved grudgingly to make room for the chair Dickon brought forward, and Drake lit his pipe slowly while the other took a bite from his square of tobacco, twisting off the tough, dark lump from the compressed cake. Jocelle sat in the rear of the room. Through the maze of her mumblings—lessons Martha had set for her—the two at the hearth would be speaking:

"It's a wonderful age, wonderful as any. Men, you'll see, will soon ride through the air."

"That's what they say."

"A craft heavier than air. I look to see one as big as

a steamship go from city to city, the same as railroad trains do."

"What fuel would you use to make the power to propel the engine?"

"Coal, sir, compressed coal."

"How do you compress it?"

"Compressed to one-tenth part its natural bulk. Ten times it's natural strength. Carried on board in tanks. That fellow Wright . . . tries to use gasoline. It'll never lift a big craft and I'll tell you for why. It hasn't got the power. When you say that, you say all. It hasn't got the strength."

Dickon spit a long brown stream of juice from his quid into the fireplace, the stream carefully timed and well executed, no part of it falling on the hearth. Jocelle remembered that it was said he had written a book. She was unnoticed, about nine or ten years old, at a small table near the hall door. She would lift in mind through the air to hover at each man's shoulder when he spoke, a bird of strong wings and sharp beak, black and invisible, going to and fro above their heads, over their breasts, including them and herself to itself, in their voices, moving with their words, never at rest, a flutter of ruffled feathers with their querulous words, a croaking cry with their protests, a pulsing of quiet wings when they brooded long over some opinion. They seemed to her, these men, ugly,

52

gnarled, and wind-torn as rock from Possum Ridge brought indoors.

"Did you read three times through your lesson?" Drake asked her when he happened once to turn toward her direction.

"I read through it only once," she answered. She continued her mumblings.

She had read it three times, but the fiction pleased her. As a child who had read the lesson but once she sat dully over the pages, savoring the delight of being a child that did not know, pretending that she could not recognize the word "October," and building around it a structure made up of oxen and briars and the odors of burning wood.

Dickon was speaking: "Helios, the old man of the sky. He gives light both for the gods and for men. He knows all. The son of Hyperion and some god-woman. I disremember the name. Sluttish stories to tell you a true physical fact."

"How do you account for intelligence?"

"Prometheus. Forethought. It's said he formed the first men out of clay. That's how man got his start. There was a long war, Prometheus and Jupiter. There was a trick in it somewheres. They made a woman to be the wife to Prometheus. Kneaded water and earth, mud pies, and made it take the shape of a woman. Shaped like the god-

53

desses. Minerva came along and gave her wisdom. Venus gives beauty and what-not. Mercury gives her a crafty nature. Trucked out with all this finery she was called Pandora, all-gifted."

Above stairs Martha worked in her chamber or, from the top of the front porch, she identified stars. She was hidden and quiet, swift and careful, given to hours of contemplation and study, with sudden gestures of kindliness and caressing. Jocelle would sniff sometimes at her smooth dark hair, liking the sweet odor that came from the soft loopings and braids.

The talk at the fireside grew remote and drowsy, a long slow account of some vehicle, some proposed engine that would leave the earth. It would be built thus and thus. A thin sheet of some light metal. Air compressed in chambers. Propelled by steam derived from compressed coal. "Next you'd want to study wind currents." The long thin stream of brown juice cut the air as an arc and went safely home to the ashes. "I take notice a heap of how the wind blows. It's my belief the air flows in layers. All the noise and bluster is down near the earth."

"Yes, I reckon as much."

"You'd ride with me, I know. Never touch terra firma. Move in the ethereal element. Go up like a balloon off the roof. Come back to roost. You'll ride with me yet."

"It's not worth a continental damn."

"Why?"

"You build an engine?"

"Well, you wait and see, sir."

"I wouldn't give a rotten turnip for your machine to fly with."

"It's not for sale, nohow."

"It's not worth a continental damn."

A swift thin arc shot toward the fireplace. A brown comet of liquid shot forth in a swift arc of protest to fall into the red flame of the sun made by the burning coals. "It's a sound principle . . ."

"You try to build without mathematics. God's sake! What a grindstone! What a lumber! A piece of plunder! A clumsy two-wheeled jackass cart. A bitch's wagon to fetch turnips out of a rag-picker's garden. A billygoat cart to haul tin cans off the dumps in Louisville."

When Jocelle was in her thirteenth year, she had come upon her, as a slowly growing appearance or a vision, a knowledge of truth, of the truth. It came first as if it were a mental apparition, undefined, but with it came a wish or a will or a desire. She wanted to have this which she imperfectly sensed or conceived; she determined that she would have it. Candor appeared to her, as divided from secrecy. Later, after the passion for truth came, she grew into some partial knowledge of what truth might be, gathering this from what lay around her, seeing Martha

55

speak to her grandfather, telling what she had done exactly regardless of the blame that might follow. Seeing Drake set numbers into a book, being careful to have each right, she kept a secret passion to speak the truth, a will and a desire upwelling within her to have the truth plainly in her hands and to move among things that were plainly reported. With the desire for truth came a desire to level herself to the level of this certain, untarnished, clear report that lay all about her. Wanting no distinction beyond that which the truth gave, she delighted in truth-telling. She saw then that J.T., when he came, reported each thing carefully, seeming careless of the matter, as if truth were an ordinary occurrence.

She learned to say many of the commonly known lyric poems of the language, wanting to have some share in what Martha knew. "I want to learn only the true ones," she said.

"I'm not sure I know which are always . . ." Martha said, falling into a reverie.

She learned "The Rime of the Ancient Mariner." Hearing her chant the ballad, Drake cried out:

"Mathematics, young woman, what's it for?"

He set her to work through a book and he found the mistakes in her sums, in her multiplications. The simpler fundamentals of algebra followed. Remembering the poems, Jocelle thought that this new science also made a pretty page. Drake viewed his barnyard from the com-

pleted bridge or the lookout. He stood here in the sun
or the wind, directing, seeing for himself that his cows
were properly tended. Jocelle took her slate there to work
out her difficulty, to have it approved when finished. His
loud shouts and his demands flowed about the rear wall
of the house. Each calf was known to him, for as soon as
it was born it was brought, with the mother, to the near-
est enclosure below and there he carefully noted it.

"Do you ever hear from Catharine?" he asked Jocelle.
She was thirteen years old.

"Once since she left. She didn't tell me where she lived.
Three years now since she wrote," she replied, the truth
blossoming.

If a child were brought from town, Rose or Celia, there
would be no lessons while the visit lasted. When Martha
was reading from Latin poets, Jocelle began to inflect the
Latin paradigms and later she read of the Gallic wars. Or
they would gather eggs from the hen-runs or go far across
the fields to look for a lost turkey. Martha played the
piano, her playing becoming each year more exact and
fine.

"She'd better go to a seminary," she said of Jocelle.

"When she's turned sixteen," Drake answered her.

Jocelle knew that Martha loved someone who lived far
away, whom she met only when she went from Wolflick.
The name of this person was never spoken. But at length
she induced Martha to call the name. They searched for a

book in the book-shelves in the upper hallway, and not finding it there, they looked among the piles of torn books in the attic above the second floor. Leaning together, searching as if they were of one mind, as if one pair of eyes looked into the cluttered papers and worn volumes, Jocelle whispered:

"What was the name of her lover?"

"It was John Ridd, my dear."

"You've got a lover yourself. What's his name too?"

And the whispered answer came: "His name is Wayne."

III

O N A soft autumn day when the sunshine was dispersed broadly from a seashell-opalescent sky, Jocelle, with Martha as guardian, went to the seminary she was to attend. Arriving at last by a carriage that conveyed passengers from the railway station, they came to the place in mid-afternoon.

All around were the great trees that were fresh from recent rains. The red building which was the boarding hall spread through maple boughs and arose above with a gray slated roof. When the carriage stopped at the low step-stone, and while Jocelle looked about her, a bell inside chimed softly, and almost at once a bevy of girls came skipping or running, fast or slow, spreading outward from a wide doorway, and she quivered and sobbed with joy at the sight of them, assuming a part with them while they yet ran lightly over the pavement. They gave no attention to the vehicle across the space of entrance paving, but they spread and ran forward as if they were a flock of small birds fluttering to a feeding ground. They tossed their curls or they pulled small wool caps over their heads. They flung bright wool jackets about their shoulders or tossed them in the air, running now across the farther banks of green, become a panel that might at any moment become fixed in any one of its lovely designs. They were shouting thin musical cries as they ran:

"I'll take Josephine!"

"Mary Bell, Sue, Annie Fink!"

"You can take two, not three!"

"Two, two, not three!"

"Annie Fink and Laurie May!"

"Sue, then, and Mary Bell!"

Some contests had begun, even in the choosing of the names. They ran farther away on the grass, spreading over a wide green, shouting and tossing a large ball. Jocelle passed beyond a tall white pillar and entered the door of the house, walking behind Martha.

Later from an upper window Jocelle saw the girls far out on the green running forward and back with long crooked sticks in their hands, beating another ball here and there. Their cries came as a high fine singing, unevenly beating, stillness and cry and the multiplied cheers of the victors. At sundown they came back across the open space, walking in twos and threes, coming toward her, and she knew that they were coming to assume her to their groups, their laughter, and work and play. Shrinking, she watched them from the window in an ecstasy of ful-

60

filled being, wanting the morrow, wanting Martha to be gone so that she could begin to live thus, to be one of the bright wool caps that walked toward the house now, that passed out of her sight beneath the pediment below her room.

The girls were assembled each day in a white hall where classes in reading, in Latin, in sciences, were taught. As they came in at the door, one after another, or two or three together, they walked in no order but that brought about by their choice in walking together or apart. Jocelle was younger than the others, but Martha had taught her well and she held a high place. Through the halls ran a sweet unrelated jargon of piano- and violin-playing, scales, phrases, chords, or on Mondays came sweet blended choruses that mingled with the chilling drafts of the floors and corridors, through the upreaching flights of stairs and the down-tripping feet of many girls. Jocelle had a great delight in the hymns and choruses, in the far-echoing chanting, half heard and half lost, that came when hymns were practiced in the chapel. Then in a trance she wrote algebraic forms on a blackboard or she translated absently at troubled passages of the *Æneid,* for she had not known singing beyond her duets with Martha.

She lived in the boarding hall for the girls and came and went to the high-pitched laughter and shrill interchanges of her fellows. There would be hours for evening study, reference books to be searched down from hiding on the shelves, soft white fingers running across the rims of the leaves to flutter at last to the wanted fact. No rough voice called from an outer balcony or bridge admonishing men in the practices of cattle. No sour old hounds slept by an open fire. After dinner the bright lights burned in the recreation hall, and some girl would clatter a run of dance music at the piano. The girls would dance together then, and new dances would be learned, the fox-trot and the difficulties of the tango shared amid lightness and laughter, anticipating some greater event when young men would be at hand. When the hour was at end, the lights would suddenly twinkle and then burn dim, a signal from the dean that the time for study had come.

"What's 'ambidexterous'?" There would be serious need beneath the query.

"Means able to use his left hand equal to his right."

"Means more'n that. Means he's right-handed in his left hand."

"Means he's right-handed on both sides."

"A fish is ambidexterous."

"What's a poly-dexterous?"

"Like a thousand-leg."

Knowledge was held in common. Nobody stinted or

hoarded or concealed. Superiority came through an ability to retain, for all ideas flowed freely and were shared openly. The more feeble vessels let the learning leak away through their weak containers or overflow their shallows.

Letters would come infrequently from Martha, now far away as lost in some other dream. She was in the place where her lover of some former time now stayed. She had studies that took her to the lectures on solar eclipses. There was something of the Milky Way, dropped in passing, as proof of a busy week and a happy climax when some eminent authority and discoverer had talked to a small group. Jocelle, reading thus, went once to her window to look out briefly at the stars, the reality of which had been forgotten, and she waved a light hand toward them, crying: "By George, there's old cosmos. Drat all Jupiter!" laughing: "I'll see you later."

"She's got a cousin at Bigwig University."

"She's got a cousin is a great wizz."

Arms would be twined around her, skipping away with her feet over the light snow to the White Hall.

"I always like to sit close to any girl has got a cousin is a wizz."

"Maybe she's my cousin; she's my aunt!"

They would make a song of it to cry with their class racket, making variations:

"Maybe he's my brother; he's my grandpa."

"Maybe he's my Poppa; he's my friend."

63

The girls of her class seemed lovely, soft, sweet creatures of delicate hands and carefully tended hair. There were close dark curls that nestled against a shoulder. The girl of the red hair had fine soft skin and a crumpled mouth that took on infinite movements when she spoke or smiled. They were of blond hair or brown, dimple cheek or plain, straight brows or knotted; they went about in twos or threes; they kept secrets together. Now and then one would seem to put on deeper marks of adolescence, as if, unnoticed, the acts of growth had leaped forward at this point. This was recognized only when a new frock revealed the form beneath it in lines that had been overlooked in the old familiar dress. A leap here and a vague movement there, and they, all together, went forward in maidenhood.

"Who said: 'Thou canst not speak of that thou canst not feel'?"

" 'Dost not feel,' it is."

"Look in the book."

"What book?"

"Look in *Romeo* . . ."

"Oh, thanks."

"A word to the wise."

"Rosalee is going to have her hair clipped."

"No, no . . ."

"Have a Castle-clip. Yes, I am."

"Will your mamma let you?"

"I'm off the bottle."

"Do you believe it? What she said, 'dost not feel'?"

"No . . . yes, I guess."

"I can speak of a—of a hornet . . ."

"Go easy now, Annie Fink."

Through her sense of the experimental music that was forgotten, its discords, falling sweetly unblended through the halls, of gentle professors who admonished kindly and praised her well for work sufficiently done, she saw herself as reflected and reflecting endlessly, her life pitched now to the gentle fervor of the girls, her mates. Herself in her glass where her bright brown hair shone, brushed each evening until it glistened, bound by day with a bright ribbon fillet and put on her head in braid or up-pinned curls, she would carry the image. The girls wore peach-basket hats in the spring.

"Say, she's got a beautiful mouth."

"Whose mouth?"

"Annie Fink's."

"Jocelle too."

They watched one another above the strength of pulling and thrusting arms in a game. Mouths were defended or criticized, as were hands and hair and feet, ankles and arms and knees. "It's no matter what the shape is," Annie Laurie said, "a mouth, I mean. So it twinkles when a girl talks." The young men at a neighboring college thus had something to do with this report. Preparations for the spring contests in the games came swiftly then. The year was passing. Reviews in classes were searching and teachers were sometimes dismayed at what had been forgotten. The study hall became popular and books for review were searched from the shelves. A girl, in a maze of facts and application:

"Last night I fell into a wonderment."

"What did you wonder?"

"I was on my way home from the hothouse. I felt the ground go down under my feet like a cushion while I walked. That made me wonder. It was nearly supper time. Dark outside. My feet went in whenever I stepped, but my body floated along even, on a level all the time. My heart ran evenly in a straight line, and my shoulders. It was after that I fell into a wonderment."

"When you went up to your room, I reckon."

"I sat down beside the window and looked out. I couldn't tell what day it was nor what year nor even my own name. I wondered who discovered Asia. Who Europe? They always say Columbus discovered America. 'Was America the only one?' I asked. I wondered why they never put it in the history who . . ."

"I reckon the supper-gong broke a hole in your wonderment and let sense in."

Jocelle always thought of one of the young men from the college as passing before a thronged grandstand, as beating time to the cheers of a hundred college fellows, as gay, debonair, and lovely, the cheer-leader at a game. His name was Miles Patterson. He would toss bright greetings toward the girls from the seminary, standing before his class, reflecting for his men their fervor for victory, the maestro playing on the instrument of their assembled being. He was quick and graceful in bearing. His gestures as he had assembled the cries of his men and brought them to rhythmic order in class-jargonings were a dance of arms and shoulders, of a body moving in stylized agility. His gestures were for the men; he drew noise and rhythm out of them with his lifted hand. For the girls all the while were inquiries, his capricious asking for favor, for their approval of what he did with his men. Jocelle thought of this one with a shy, delicate fervor, scarcely calling his name in her thought. The end of the year was at hand. There were hurried preparations in the boarding hall, borrowed wreaths, sashes, trinkets, the girls running from room to room in the dusk. It was the evening of the dance. Names were understood in the flickering of an eye or the borrowing of a ribbon.

"If he so much as looks at me, I'll ask no more. I'll die of dclight," one said.

"Oh, Rosalee, suppose he's not even here."

"Eddie might not even come."

67

The recreation hall was a ballroom. The floor reflected the dozen brilliant lights, and a screen of palms hid the three or four musicians who ran the music swiftly from one-step to fox-trot. There were games played with bright balls tossed on ribbons. A continual preparation for some event that might follow, that continually lingered unfulfilled; it seemed thus to Jocelle as she glided in and out of the dances. Her dress, sent by Martha, was rose-pink, with pleatings that gathered darkly to deep rose, and the tightly drawn skirt with its hem flutings kept her limbs bounded so that she glided lightly, moving as one muscle on a pair of closely related slippers.

In a maze of paper lanterns carried by the girls and boys, the throng surged and broke into couples to march out through the wide doorway to the porch and over the pavement to the farther green. Jocelle marched with Patterson, and their lanterns made a pink glow on their faces. They admired the pink and silver flowers on her bright paper globe as they walked. They led the long trail of faint fire over the close-cropped grass, making the pattern for the rest, walking before, doubling the design in a long thread that trembled, that fluted in and out through the soft June dark. They talked of where they would be the next year, not knowing, being vaguely afraid of the unknown.

"Anyway, I'll still be Jocelle."

"And I'll be Miles."

68

Walking thus, and in delight, they went before in the midnight procession, going with their dim paper lanterns into the dark lawn.

Back to Wolflick: The girls being gone from Jocelle's presence, they were seen pleasantly in memory, were arranged in design as seen from the beginning when they fluttered from the doorway to their games on the green. Martha came back at the beginning of August, and Jocelle entered acutely into Martha's coming. The fields and hills of Wolflick were slightly unfamiliar, as stretching farther than she had remembered, and Jocelle knew that the stillness of the country came to Martha as a presence that spread about her. She caught the smile from Martha's brightened eyes, and they went happily about the house, which they put into its best and most pleasant order, the old piano dusted and rubbed until it shone, the china vases from the day of Joan filled with bouquets from the kitchen garden or from the fields. She found herself pausing to hear the faint noises that came into the stillness of the mid-day hours when the animals drowsed and there was no clamor from the stable-yards, hearing for herself, and again as Martha heard. They would laugh at the harsh jargon that came now and then, interchange between the bridge and the stable-pens. Martha's passion seemed everywhere present. They would walk out through the avenue among the scattered trees of the front pasture and meet the postman at the roadside box. Jocelle waited now before Martha.

"Oh, will there be a letter? Today, will it . . . ?" She would not be the first to touch the missive, however, standing back, having opened the box, waiting before the onrush of passion that caught the letter in hand but was too surcharged to read it understandingly for several hours.

Martha kept a picture of Wayne hidden in her desk, to be taken out when she sat near, to be put carefully behind the lock when she went away. Jocelle listened to accounts of this man in a fog of self-forgetting. The words, the ideas expressed, the chains of experience behind the utterance, came with a continual sense of the enormous physical power of a man who had thus, indirectly, spoken. His strong body leaped up within his garments, his hand sweeping the air, his large frame suddenly realized, so that opinion seemed alive with a presence. Even though she could not hold to the opinions long, knowing herself to be adolescent and incompetent, the power of it rushed toward her and stunned her thought so that she swam in momentary floods of acquiescence. Martha would be singing:

"A knight comes riding, riding,
  To one in danger biding. . . ."

Jocelle was in the parlor before a waning fire. Sitting on a low stool, she was mentally on tiptoe to realize all that Martha knew in raptures and agonies and fears. Martha had gone on her horse to the farther end of the farm. She would ride in a canter over the withering turf of the pasture, scarcely touching ground in the tread of the little mare. She would be greeting the twilight stars as they came into the pale sky, making delighted phrases with which to name them, singing the smooth, romantic song of the riding knight as she had it in the making, and supplying with her tra-la-la what the song lacked. Jocelle left the fire and went to the upper rear of the house and out on the bridge to watch for the rider, knowing in part all that the rider knew.

At the top of the pasture, near the gate that led from the woodlot behind the cabin, the laborers Wade and Elkins were butchering a hog. A great kettle stood over a smoldering fire and a mist of vapor arose as from a caldron. The men were cutting the flesh with long knives and, apart, the dogs were growling over their share. Through the frosty dusk flowed the red light from the smoldering firebrands under the kettle, so that the faces of the dark people who worked there were illuminated and their bodies were distorted, their feet stepping in and out of the bright glow, into the twilight and back again to the firelight, where they were enhanced and enlarged to be the feet of giants at work on some vast creative purpose

71

that had to do with the slaying of swine, as if the spirit of a planet were being slowly liberated by this murderous rite.

Martha left her horse at the stable and let it find its way to a stall after she had removed the saddle and hung it on the pegs beside the cornroom, Jocelle leaving the bridge, knowing what Martha did. Martha walked forward from the rear of the stable, past the men who were blocking meat out of the dead swine, their strong arms and earnest faces bent now as if they proved some lesson in planetary anatomy. Going from the bridge, Jocelle left them in the last glow of the twilight, hearing their musical flare of replies and commands, hearing their sharp, musical admonitions to the woman who carried the titbits away for safe housing.

All around was the speech of the country, and this again added continually to the heightened reality as it called their attention and awakened their admiration, even affection, for what lay about. The speech was their own, Martha's and Jocelle's, but in the interval of Martha's absence it had on her tongue become flat and crisp. Here among the lightly rolling hills it rolled lightly, spoken from relaxed throats, and there was always time for each slow vowel, for each sung diphthong. The muscles below the lower lips were let droop over certain consonants, a habitual facial gesture that halfway induced a smile or suggested smiling, so that the imitative response was a

72

faint smile. Into this fluid speech would come forceful words, strong old utterance that leaped out of the yielding medium.

Two were speaking in the kitchen as she passed, Mrs. Wright and some relative of hers who had come to spend a night. Of someone:

"Shoes made him so sore all over his feet he coulden't hardly walk, and that's why he leaves off shoes so much and goes bare. It's said his feet stay well ever since he left off his shoes."

"Shut the door to."

"I'm under a doubt whether I put the salt in the bread."

"You put it in. I saw your hand go inside the jar whilst you told how Jack Briggs, it's said, took to preachen."

In the diningroom before the fire, a large hound fitfully sleeping to the left of the fireplace under the cabinet where the guns were kept. A voice was speaking, droning steadily forward, Stoner Drake instructing his overseer, Abe Wright.

"Soon after sunup, and I want Wade out with the mules to plow the old field. Let Elkins pile the brush at the foot of the hillside where the plantbed will be next year. Don't be in a mighty hurry. There's no call to rush things through and halfway do. I culled over the seed grain myself and took out the most of the trash. . . ."

Martha would be coming then into the parlor where Jocelle was standing before the grate fire, she, Jocelle,

73

knowing that her slim body showed as a shadow through her dress, as if her bones were visible through shadowed flesh. She had grown tall in the past year; she had become suddenly a person to be counted in the house. She now saw that Martha half shrank from telling her, as she had already guessed, that Wayne would come there, thinking that the words, "Wayne is coming," would call for some more full explanation than she could give to a child that had suddenly grown tall and had taken the stature of a woman without having a woman's mind and passion. But she saw then that while Martha's shrinking lasted she abruptly reversed her mental state, emptied it with a thought of Jocelle as a girl haunted by loyalties and devout with womanly feelings. Holding fast to this picture and seeing the tender and empty yearning on the other's face, she said quickly:

"Wayne is coming. Here. To see me. He'll be here tomorrow."

"Oh, jimminy!"

"You can help me."

"Why didn't you tell? Why didn't you say-so sooner?"

"It's been in the air a long while."

"I'll bake you some little round cakes with raisins on the top. . . . I'll hunt for a blanket for his bed. We'll make his bed up in the west room. I looked today to see was there another blanket anywhere in the house and I couldn't find but the brown one with the blue stripe."

74

"We are an ill-balanced house. Fourteen or sixteen rooms and two blankets."

"A grand piano and about four pillow cases."

"Better'n four, but no great abundance."

"You can have my saddle. To ride together. I hope Elkins can spare you a horse. If Wayne can really ride, there's old Clipper. It's such a fine thing to have company come here."

She was standing before the waning fire and her body was partly chilled by the coolness of the room, the corners of which were never warmed in winter. The near-frost crept toward her and sent envoys to beat light trills and quavers at her nerve-ends, but such was her inner warmth that the chill was for the most part shed. She danced a few steps and shuffled on the bare floor before the fireplace.

"If there's not a sheet, I'll give Wayne mine and I'll sleep on the old silk piano cover we don't use any more. And when the visit's over, I'll ask again to have some sheets bought. Tell how long Wayne might stay and tell again what kind he is and what kind of hair and eyes. I'll be all cumfluttered to have a man come to visit us."

Jocelle beside her, Martha told Drake that Wayne would be coming to stay three or four days. He accepted the fact with grace and said after a little:

"Tell Elkins to go to one of the creek farms, Lanham's, and get some ducks. We'll have a duck supper. This place is always empty of good fowls. Look and see if there's one more cask in the cellar. God Almighty! Is company a matter to shudder the heart of a Drake? Let him stay downstairs in the west room here across from the parlor. Let a fire be built there two days before he comes. What's he here for, this fellow Wayne, you said his name was? Who is he? What's his object in life?"

"He is one of my friends." Martha made a long speech, talking around the fact of Wayne's friendship, saying that she had known him in the university. He studied sciences but he liked poetry, liked human thought and speculation. She thought on careful consideration that he liked best to study peoples and races of men, to study their languages. He had a tender sense of language as being some essence from the roots of human life. She feared that she had said too much in saying this, and she amended the statement, saying that he was tolerant of people in whatever they fancied or held as important, and that he was not too ambitious, not ambitious in any usual sense. He cared more to know a thing than to have it, she thought. She knew his mother and one of his sisters, for they often came to stay with him through a winter term. She wanted him to see her country in the winter.

Martha stopped speaking, and Jocelle, seeing that she was afraid, wanted to say that Wayne was merely a friend, wanted to cry out against some hostility which she saw arising against the near relation which the visit seemed to imply. She remembered on the instant the letter which was locked in the desk in Martha's room, a letter which Martha had not yet endured to read entirely, and so she joined Martha in silence, standing near her beside the door.

"He's welcome, right welcome," Drake said heartily, after the silence had endured several minutes. "Let him come. Tell Elkins to groom a horse. If there's a thing here for a learned man to see, show him all around the place."

The guest came at supper time, brought from Anneville in a horse-drawn carriage. Supper passed with formal pleasantness and reserve, the meats carefully served from the head of the lengthened table. The wine was poured for the men from a long green decanter into the little squat crimson-tinted glasses, where it glowed if the light from one of the well-polished oil lamps fell upon it. After supper all went to the parlor and sat in a large half-circle before the high coal fire. Drake sat near the center of the room.

The guest seemed not yet to have offered a reason for their heightened being. Jocelle sat near the piano, divided from the others by the large frame of the instrument that reflected the warmth and brightness of the blazing fire. Martha seemed beautiful to Jocelle in her dress of dark wool that had a glint of soft shell-pink drapery to line the flowing collar. Walter, their cousin, who had come the day before, brought the book of family photographs from a table and searched it for likenesses of themselves, and underneath his banter was revealed a genuine respect and admiration for the pictured faces he found there. Drake smiled faintly, sitting upright in his large, stiff chair, his arms folded frequently across his breast.

"Have you seen a comet, young man?" he asked.

The visitor expected to see one through a large glass in the spring. The fire rippled and made long lambent flames of tenuous matter that lay momentarily as comet tails against the black of the chimney or disappeared into the sooty flue, and Drake told of the great comet of 1834 as report of it had come down from his grandfather. It was thought to be the bringer of pestilence and war and famine, and all around people were dying of cholera. In the household of one Drake, uncle to his father, thirty-three persons died, blacks and whites all told. "Pestilence and war and famine," he said. "And now war in Europe under way. Pestilence and war and famine . . ." Everyone present knew the nature of his vow and knew that he regarded this hour but lightly, that he upheld the forms of a house and the dignity of a family, the uses of the parlor, but that he regarded them as of little account beside the defiance in his frame. Jocelle sat in the niche made by the black arc of the piano and the hearth. Her dress, of a soft pearl-white silk, a garment left from her year at the seminary, being slightly outgrown, scarcely covered her

78

limbs as the parlor demanded, and it made of her, thus, a child, ill-covered and not regarded, an intense watcher of the scene. The guest fitted but a little way into the drama before her. He seemed amused but withdrawn, a man of a large frame, a large face indented with a deep line on either cheek.

"I'd like to know, young man," Drake continued, "after you've looked at the comet through this large telescope, and after you've made some notations and observations on the spectrum, after you cogitate this wandering luminary, I'd like to know what you think it's made of and what for, and where it originated. Was it, I want to know, thrown off by the sun or by some of the major planets? That's all I want to know."

Wayne was embarrassed at this demand. He shut his mouth together tight, and the deep indentations of the cheeks sank deeper. He crossed his knees and locked his hands between them, as if he would preserve himself, thus, entire. He spoke slowly: "You ask a good deal of an amateur whose interests are divided among several matters." He looked away from Martha altogether, gazing at the bright reflection of the fire in the black marble of the hearth.

"Enlightenment is what we want here," Drake said.

"We'll get ourselves a telescope," Martha said. She got up from her chair, and Wayne rose to stand beside his seat. "I am going to play," she continued, "will I?" Wayne continued to stare at the reflected flame and she passed behind Drake's chair. "What will I play, Jocelle? I haven't played twice all month, the keys have been so cold."

"Play Bach," Jocelle said with her lips, scarcely making a sound.

"Enlightenment enough, Bach," Martha half whispered, a sob in her breath.

In the frost of the early morning Martha and Wayne were walking out to the stables to be mounted and off for a ride. Jocelle, already among the horses, was directing Elkins in preparing the equipment. "Two good bridles, Elkins . . . take the throat-latch off this one and shift it over to the clean bit." Putting together the best the stable had, she contrived good bridles for both horses. By the time the two riders had come across the paddock, she had each horse well saddled and bridled, groomed to his best appearance, and brought to the stable door.

"The angel of the stable," Martha said, making a genuflection toward Jocelle. The piecing out had been recognized and appreciated. Martha was in a bright humor and the morning was gray with bright luminous frost.

"What way will you go?" Jocelle asking, and Martha replied, her hand flung about in a maze: "This way and then that and off yonder and up again. I'm going to lose Wayne out of his cardinal points he's so proud of."

And Wayne, on his horse, the pose of an equestrian marble: "I'm never lost. I'm here, now, me," and to Martha: "Me and you. North, south, east, and west can go to the devil."

Two blasts from the horn came from the wall of the house behind them, a stout thrust of sound that came roughly into the radiant gray of the morning, and Wade dropped the axe he had been grinding and hurried away toward the woodlot.

"I told you how you drove that peg crooked," Elkins called after him.

Jocelle and the horn were alike already forgotten by the two riders, who were holding some intimate and eloquent controversy.

"I'm glad I'm here," Wayne was saying.

"Oh, glad! . . . But last night you were afraid."

There was low half-whispering and laughter. They rode away side by side into the October whitefrost, moving with the movements of their beasts that kept together in an uneven gait, his hand on her hand that was free of the bridle.

When they were gone, Jocelle went aimlessly over the house, or she set the parlor in order, bringing boughs of bright leaves for the vases. She would wander to the window to look for the return. Something had been subtracted from her with the departure of the lovers, and she could not follow them in mind or see where they would be at any moment riding. In thought she went, hour after hour, more minutely into their meanings to try to dissect their delights. Failing to comprehend by this study in anatomy, she sank into a half-dream on a divan in the parlor, letting all life slip past her, craving to understand nothing. Falling asleep, she waked suddenly with a clear vision of passion, of joy, of human delights as derived from interchanges with another. The appearance was so vivid that her first thought was that the absent had returned, that they had come into the room. She rose quickly and went to the south porch to look forward across the pasture.

Late in the day there were frequent blasts blown from the summoning horn. Wade and Elkins were called again and again. A question was flung down from the bridge. Anger poured over the order given for the better disposal of the cattle. The strong step sounded again and again on the stair. Lights were wanted in the early gloom. The house was illuminated, as in preparation, every light tended and trimmed, replenished with oil. Jocelle was called to assist in making ready the lights. She set a lamp in the guest's room and another at Drake's elbow, one in his bedroom across the way, and one in the parlor before a window. The dark of the night came swiftly.

It was later when a murmur of speech and laughter, mingled with the slow tread of the horses, came from the driveway. Voices called from the paddock. Martha seemed unfatigued by the long day. Her dark hair was caught neatly under her small hat and her face was bright with assured pleasure, her cheeks pink from the cold dusk. She entered the diningroom, laughing with her lover. Jocelle was bringing cups to the table where Drake sat at the head of the board. Walter was not there. Drake was eating slowly as if he had been at the table for a long time. Jocelle was afraid. She had not come to sit at the table.

The rough voice broke in its terrible accusations the moment Martha and Wayne came through the door. They were accused of evil. The swiftness of the speech that hurled term after term without coherence did not obscure the meaning Drake wished to convey. He made clear his opinion. The two were waved back from the table.

"Go eat with the hogs in the trough," he said. "But see you keep clear of the manger where my horses go."

His meaning went swiftly to Martha. She stopped quickly and looked at him in terror, crying out: "No, no!"

"Go eat with the hogs, I say. A whore and a whore-catcher. Go on. Go take your harlotry out into the bushes." He leaned forward in his chair, speaking and gesturing.

They went away by the outer door, but Jocelle remained weeping in the farther corner. He answered her whimpering with further accusation, muttered and spent. "Go on," he said, and she left by the door to the hallway. Martha and Wayne were at the front door. She was sitting on a bench shuddering as in a chill, but he walked at the farther side

83

by the rail as if he were angry. "I will not stay, I'll go with you, wherever you go," Martha was saying, but he did not reply to this while he walked back and forth, cursing the day, or he wiped his hands with his handkerchief.

"My things, my bag," he said. "I won't go inside. They can stay where they are and rot. . . . I'll never go inside."

Martha was crying for pity. "I make apology. I ask for nothing but pity . . . understanding." Jocelle offered to get for him his things, seeing that he would otherwise leave them, and she went to the west room and packed his bag swiftly. They stood apart, speaking. "I can't stay," Martha said, and she was shivering with exhaustion now. There was nothing more to be said. They were repeating. She declared that she would not stay, but he made no response to this.

"It is for me consummated," he said at last. "There is nothing more to it. It's all forgiven and forgotten. It's ten years afterward as far as I am concerned."

He took the bag Jocelle had brought. With a nod of the head toward Jocelle he looked away from Martha, away from the house altogether. He pulled his hat forward on his brow and walked away down the carriage-road, seen going swiftly in the dim light, past the pond and toward the far hedge.

Martha recovered slowly from the shock of that night. After fever and delirium she was entirely deaf for many

84

weeks. Isolated from all sounds, she had written messages from Jocelle, until at length the noises of the farm came back to her, at first the loud horn and the screaming of the swine. By the time the swallows were fluttering into the chimney again, she could hear the low whispered thunder of their wings.

IV

THE COLD settled each week more near and became a solid medium that fixed itself upon the farms. The tobacco hung in the barn for curing and the corn had been gathered from the shocks. The apples that had been gathered through the early weeks of the month were brought now to the grassy space west of the cabin to be picked over and put aside for storing. Mrs. Tobin, wife of the newly employed overseer of the fields, went steadily through the task, for to her the apples were a labor begun, half-done, or done. Jocelle knelt beside the mound of fruit, helping with the task, and she chose the fine apples with pride, as if she were rewarded by their goodness. She saved two handsome apples, the largest of the heap, meaning to eat one herself and to give the other as a prize to someone, she knew not whom, for they were two shapely sound fruits, the skin deeply red over a golden underglow, and on the stem of one clung a russet leaf.

While the work of the apples went forward into the falling twilight, a stranger walked up through the avenue from the road. He passed beside the house and came to the space by the wall of the cabin where the apple heap lay. He greeted Mrs. Tobin as one who knew her, calling her "Miss Nettie," and he remembered later to remove his hat, which he held, turning it about in his hands.

"Ain't you Preacher Briggs?" Mrs. Tobin asked.

"Brother Briggs, I am. Jack Briggs, or some call me Johnnie Briggs. Farmhand or preacher, whichever you'd rather."

He was dressed in dark, unmatched garments that had been faded to a near sameness by the rain. The dust of the road lay heavily in the wrinkles of his sleeves. His smile was strange, lingering continually at one side of his mouth and reaching back toward the left side of the jaw, where it showed beneath his thin short reddish beard. He seemed humble, turning his hat about anxiously, as if he were afraid. There was an odor of beasts, such as sheep, about him.

"God bless you and all in the house," he said.

"You are very welcome," the woman said, nervously.

"God bless you," he said to Jocelle.

She gave him one of the apples she had chosen. He took the fruit and smiled broadly upon her. He began to eat the apple hungrily, seeming not to notice its beauty of color or form. Large bites of the apple floated loosely about in his mouth, the juices running.

"Did you want to see somebody?" Nettie Tobin asked. "Tobin, maybe?"

88

He finished the apple and threw the core far from him. He had put the hat back upon his head.

"What does he want?" Tobin asked, coming near.

"Man, sir, how do you do?" the stranger said.

"I know his name but I can't call it to mind," Tobin replied.

"Jack Briggs, 'tis, God bless you."

"He could cut some wood," Mrs. Tobin said, "for his supper. The men were so busy all day there's not hardly any cut. Let him cut kindling for a spell."

The stranger replied to this. "Let us pray," he said. He lifted his hand and, having taken off his hat, he began his prayer.

"While the earth remaineth, seedtime and harvest, and cold and heat, and summer and winter, and day and night shall not cease. . . . And the fear of you and the dread of you shall be upon every beast of the earth, and upon every fowl of the air, upon all that moveth upon the earth, and upon all the fishes of the sea; into your hand are they delivered. Every moving thing that liveth shall be meat for you; even as the green herb have I given you all things.

"Amen."

The Tobins spoke no more of the wood. Tobin began to carry the baskets of apples to the cellar under the kitchen, plodding with basket after basket.

"I have heard it said the man of this house is a pent-up man," the stranger said.

"It's true he goes his own way," Tobin replied, stopping a moment in his labor. "He goes alone."

"That he won't set a foot on the earth."

This was granted as true.

"It's a strange life," the preacher said.

"No man would dare say so much to Stoner Drake. It's been a long while now since any offered to tell him so."

"I'm here to preach to Stoner Drake. I'm here to preach him back outen hell if he's so headed."

"Don't say I let you go in," the woman said. "If you go it's by your own right. It's not for me to take any inside."

Jocelle went to the diningroom, where she lit the lamp and found for Drake his evening pipe. Back and forth from the kitchen, she saw the stranger come in. He sat near the open fire and rested as if he were weary from walking far. Later he removed his shoes, and as he walked over the bare floor, his feet made a heavy patting sound. He took from beneath a table a small piggin, as if he knew well its use. When he had put water into this, cold and hot mixed, he carried the vessel to his place beside the fire and began to wash his feet. He dried the flesh by holding his hands and feet to the fire, rubbing them meanwhile. His skin was red and warm, glowing with blood. When he had put on his shoes again, he said:

"I will go in now and speak to the man of the house."

Nettie Tobin went through the pantry to the dining-room, where Drake sat before the fire. "There's a man here, says he wants to see you," she began, as if she knew nothing of what might follow, but before she had secured a reply, the stranger, coming close behind her, began to speak.

"God bless you and all in the house," he said.

"How's that?" Drake asked.

Jocelle left the fireside and stood at the rear of the room, ready to leave if violence should appear. The stranger walked slowly to the hearth at the right of the fire and he bowed toward Drake, folding his hands nervously to-gether. A smile played continually beside his mouth. His eyes were pale gray in the bright light of the fire, and his clothes were soiled and much worn. A faint odor of some beast moved outward from him.

"You are a tramp, I take it," Drake said.

"Iffen a tramp is a walker, then it's a tramp I am. I go my way and no man does me any hurt, or iffen he does, my hand is strong and makes a hard fist. But no man hinders me."

"Have you got any skill when it comes to a day's work? Can you strip backer? Can you shuck corn?"

"I do that kind. You see my hands here. You see the hands of a man can make his victuals and build himself a shelter. God bless you."

91

"What are you after? Sakes bless us! How long have you been loose from the poorhouse. Clear out!"

Admonished roughly to talk sense, the man stood nervously beside the fire, his hat held loosely in his right hand. Jocelle wanted to thrust him out at the door and have done with the strain of his presence beside the hearth, but Drake spoke sharply, thrusting his command forward with his changed posture as he moved suddenly to the edge of his chair. "Talk sense," he said.

"Mankind, I never stay at the poorhouse. I stripped backer all last week for Mr. Billie Sayer. I bespoke work at Robinson's for two weeks hence. I buried a man a Tuesday and cut a man down that hanged himself, that would be three weeks ago. God bless you and all yourn. I got a little house of my own a far piece up Gritty Creek."

"A man of property, affluent in the country. What, in the name of all that's holy, what's he here for?"

"In the name of God, amen."

"If you're not a fool, talk sense then."

"I heard it said you were a pent-up man since a long time back."

"It's true and my own business, sir."

"God bless you."

"You've got a fine flow of blab. You say you cut a man down. Who hung himself on the Ridge?"

"God bless you, it was Alvie Wheat. No trouble to you

we might now pray iffen you give consent. Let us pray."

"Jocelle!" Drake called out.

"I'm here," she said.

"I've got here a tramp friar. Come see what's to be made of this-here thing-ma-gig. With what sect are you affiliated, sir?"

"I never preach in the churches. In a man's house is where I preach. But I go to the churches to hear the discourse and I heed what I hear or cast it out as I see fit. I preached last week for old John Ferris, at the foot of his bed, and I sang three hymns for little old dried-up Bill Bedlow in his house. I wish no harm to a soul. Could we pray?"

"All right, man, step lively. Go ahead. You've got my consent to petition your maker, whatever he was or whoever he is. Go on with you."

The man prayed as he had prayed beside the kitchen door, his prayer an oracle and not a petition. When he had finished, the quiet of the room remained as he had left it with his amen, but at length Drake spoke suddenly:

"You've got a strong smell about you."

"I slept last night in a man's stable. Sickness in his house and I said I wouldn't bother his womenfolks to make me a bed."

Mrs. Tobin came dully into the room as if she had no

knowledge of the man by the fire. She began to draw the table into the center of the floor and to prepare for the evening meal. The preacher continued to stand by the hearth, his hands drooping at his sides as if he were afraid. A faint smile showed at the left of his mouth when he turned toward the light. Jocelle went back toward the door to the hall, waiting for what might follow when Drake became aware again of the tramp by the fire. After a little he spoke to Mrs. Tobin who was passing:

"Put a plate on the table for this man. Give him his supper here."

The tramp shifted his feet and passed his hat from the left hand to the right. "Mister," he said, "surely to goodness I could eat my food with the servant in the kitchen, and thanks be to you for it there. Mankind, I never in life asked to sit with the best in the house, but I'll sit gladly enough with any, so it's humankind."

A storm arose, blowing the loose shutters and whining under the doors, whistling sadly in the chimney. Nettie Tobin brought the food to the table and Jocelle gave the stranger a seat at the right of her grandfather's place. When he had asked leave, the man spoke a brief grace, the same oracle he had spoken before. After that he ate hungrily of all the food that was offered, leaning above the board as a great animal might bend to a feeding trough. His flesh

94

was red and full of life. His opened collar laid bare a strong red throat that was burnt by the sun beneath the red hair of his beard. Martha called him the red man, whispering:

"Where did you get the red man?"

When the man had appeased his great hunger and had begun to eat daintily of the food that was left, Drake spoke to him of his home.

"You say you've got a little place up Gritty Creek. Where, now, is Gritty Creek? I don't remember."

"Past Anneville and on south. A little knob-hill stands straight on end before a small matter of a ridge. Down on one side comes a branch called Goose Run. You go on past that and double on the yon side till you come to a little house painted white, a brick house, and you turn there and go again to your left. The next branch is called Gritty Creek, and it's in the Muldrough country. It's gritty, so called, because Godalmighty has laid down there a master quantity of gritty stones. Up in the head of the branch is a little house, left me by my mammy that got it from her grandpa. Iffen you ever come that way, stop and stay a night. You'll be welcome."

"Thank you," Drake said.

Martha went away as soon as she had eaten. The stranger moved nearer to the fire and, without asking further leave, he removed his shoes and held his large bare feet to the warmth. The act was performed without embarrassment;

the shoes were set carefully aside to the right of the hearth.

"Do you always bare your feet to sit of an evening?" Drake asked. "In winter?"

"Winter makes no mite of trouble to my feet, frost or cold, no matter. It was for the health of my feet I first went bare in the house. Shoes, iffen I make a habit to wear shoes always, make me so sore all over my feet I can't hardly step. God bless you."

"A matter of a pair of stockings might be remedial. Haven't you got a pair of hose somewhere?"

"God bless you."

"Since how long have you been a religioner?"

"A matter of eight years or more."

The stranger sat meekly, letting the questions search him, but asking nothing in his turn. He arose and walked out the west door, without explanation, and his bare feet struck the floor with a heavy slow patter that was like the fall of a lion's paws on the floor of his den. Returning, he sat again by the fire and spread his feet again to the warmth. Nettie Tobin was gone to the cabin across the open passage beyond the kitchen. The kitchen was shut and dark. Jocelle lit her lamp at the diningroom fire and turned the wick up and down until it burned in a soft tongue of flame. Briggs would sleep in the room above the kitchen, which was reached by the stairway that went up between walls beyond the pantry door. A small lamp on the mantel awaited his going.

"I take it you had sometime a light paralytic stroke?" Drake asked.

"It was after I got hurted in a fight. I got a blow on my head with a monkey wrench."

"Was it after that you took up religion?"

"No, sir, it was well before. It was three years ago only since I got hit with the wrench."

The preacher sat meekly answering all that was asked. Outside, the storm had waned somewhat and beat now as a steady flow of rain against the windows.

The war in Europe being a year advanced, there were armies to be fed, and much of everything that the farm could yield was wanted. Dickon had come to build a silage tank behind the cattle barn and to rebuild the barn for the tobacco. Drake made a new sequence of notes on the horn, a blast to call Jocelle to him. It was anapæstic— two short blasts and a long one: —— —— ——————. "Find Nettie," he would say to her when she appeared before him. "Call Geril." His brisk, rough step would sound through the hallway as he set upon his journey to the upper rear of the house. Each day he would stop to adjust the weights in the clock that stood in the hall not far from the diningroom door. Six, ten, a dozen times a day he would go above, over the bridge to the lookout. Or back, he would be at the hearthside shedding cold from his large frame as he settled to his stout chair for a short rest.

"Jocelle, find out what this war is. What's it for?"

"Where will I find it? How will I?"

"Find out, I say. Get the facts."

She played a little of Martha's music, Mozart, building herself a fire in the broad grate with the coal and wood Elkins brought for her. When Martha had walked away alone, going back across the farm toward the creek, she would contrive a summer and she would plan to have one of the girls, Annie Fink or Mary Bell, to come to stay at Wolflick. There would be flowers then in the old bed beside the east chimney, and she and Annie Fink would stay all day in the swing under the walnut tree. They would be devising something together.

But there was no other girl there. Walking past Dickon she knew herself for a slim maid, one hundred and fifteen pounds in weight, eighteen years old, slim at the hips, long round legs and slim ankles. The ground was at this time frozen without snow and the grass was brown. The wind was often high in the night.

Drake muttered as he sat by the fire. Some menace had come to his flock of sheep. He would rise suddenly and walk away through the hallway, thumping up the bare steps to the loud echo made by his footsteps. When he was gone at last through the outer door to the bridge, a gust of wind through the house, and the inside silence would follow. Outside, the sharp blast on the horn. Her own summons, and she would be following up the stairs and through the outer door, to run later to the barn or out across the pasture. She would search out the sick ewes, if they grazed, and report how they fared.

At this time J.T. came to enter into a partnership with his grandfather in producing sheep and beef cattle for the markets. Plans went forward, devised on paper under the evening lamp.

Now and then Jack Briggs would come, opening the kitchen door with humility. His feet, when they were bare, were red and dark from the cold. He would find for himself a basin of water and bathe his feet before he passed into the house.

"Good even all," he would say, entering slowly. "Amen to you, Mister Drake. Thanks to you, I'll sit here by the fire."

Late in the night Dickon and Briggs would go up the narrow stairway in the corner of the diningroom and enter the bedroom above the kitchen where two beds stood. A low murmur of prayer would run through the house while Briggs prepared himself to sleep.

"To hell with you," Dickon called once when the prayer seemed long. "Say your blasted amen and go to bed."

One night when it was exceedingly cold, Jocelle and

Martha searched out comforters for J.T. in the linen press in the upper hall. Standing together in the closet while Martha guided Jocelle's explorations among the quilts, they heard a dialogue in the kitchen bedroom. Dickon was speaking:

"What's to hinder if we take all the covers to one bed and sleep together there?"

"Mankind alive, don't make too free with my bed. Leave my covers be put where they are now."

"What's to hinder if we put all in one bed for warmth and sleep there, your covers and mine?"

"Stand back offen my bed and leave my covers be. Mankind, I'd as soon sleep with a horse than sleep with a man. Put back my covers."

Jocelle laid the table, putting the knives and forks on the board. She brought the salt and pepper dishes from the sideboard and the cups for the coffee. Large napkins were laid at each plate with steel knives and forks. Room was left for the large platter of meat that would come from the kitchen.

Dickon came near and spoke rapidly. He took something from under his coat, a hidden thing, and thrust it, a book, into her hands.

"Don't let e'er other see, you hear? My book. You can have it. I give it to you. But don't let e'er see or know."

It was a long thin book, faded and old. She read the title quickly before she thrust it from view, *The Cosmograph*. Thus on the title page:

The Cosmograph (I write about the universe). Being a dissertation of the origins of matter, of the nature of life, of the origin of Man, of Order, Figurability, Succession, Retention, of the nature of the stars.

No other at Wolflick had seen this book. Jocelle hid it in the bottom of a chest. Later, toward midnight, she read it through, skipping a number of tedious paragraphs. It was a confusion of myth and natural phenomena brought together in some scarcely evident coherence, and made to point to a thesis. The old man of the sea, the omnipresent heteromorphic universe pointing to a heteromorphism, a regard for infinite diversities, these thrown into seeming confusion by the children of Chaos who were named as Earth, Love, Erebus, and Night, and by flying reptiles of the Cretaceous period. The earth covered with a thick mantle of ice. Back, going on the stairs of old Breckon's chart, Cenozoic, Mesozoic, Paleozoic, Proterozoic, Archæozoic, gone back a billion and two hundred and sixty million years. Up and down the stairs, then, stopping with the dinosaurs, one hundred and fifty million years ago, and spreading widely to include multitudes of forms described now as lost overboard, swept off the old ship to make room for the infinite heteromorphism, the everlasting otherness of kind building on kind.

Flipping the pages to the end to find the summary, she read: "Thus we see that Man, the upstart, the prig of the universe, holds no place. Not even a cog among the wheels. The whole mechanism turns, grinding out forms to pitch them over as the engine goes humming along at a merry pace, and nothing in the whole panoply of phantasmagoria cares if he falls out or in, but you might hear a thundering guffaw on Mount Olympus when he tumbles headlong back into Chaos."

She laughed when she had finished. "The old devil," she said, "what's his name? Beelzebub. Here with us to stay awhile." She laughed drowsily, smiling at her eyes that were blue now in the mirror as lit by the failing lamp. She put the book into the bottom drawer of the chest and went to sleep amused that it should be there.

A sick ewe threatened a renewal of the old menace to the sheep that were now a great flock, increased by a hundred fine ewes that had given birth to far more than their number of lambs. Drake asked the county Farm Agent to come and give advice as to the handling of the flock and the extermination of the disease, for the county had, at that time, employed a trained man to advise the farmers. Did his functions cover the handling of sheep? Drake asked at the telephone. He muttered of this newly acquired service the county was to give to the farmers "In-

sect pests, sour meadows, foot-rot, white scours, milk fever, congested udder. Next we'll have wool-eaters to eat
one another's wool. Potassium iodide and cod-liver oil.
Prevents rickets. Let the man come on."

Later, Jocelle came down from her room, the west
chamber above stairs, answering the anapæstic call of
the horn. "Go out to the stable . . . tell J.T. . . .
The county Farm Agent has come. . . . Let him . . .
Ask . . ." Anxieties and admonitions and inquiries were
stated, Drake sitting by the slow fire. The cool air of
spring came into the room through the opened west door.
"Run to the stable. . . . Tell the man to stop here when
he goes, if he pleases."

Down through the fresh spring grass and under the intense green of the new leaves she passed. The men were
gathered in the middle doorway, where the ailing sheep
were penned. J.T. was bending with the Farm Agent over
the sick ewe, and the veterinary was coming from the flowing water pipe with a large bottle in his hand. She knew
that J.T. was aware of her as having come with a message.
His manner, his lifted hand, said to her: "In a moment
. . . this is tedious . . . wait a second."

The life of the sheep was less to them than the curing
of the disease. Tobin was holding the sheep down, resting himself on the sick animal's back. The stranger bent
over the head of the sheep. His ear seemed large against
the wool that was spread beyond it. He relaxed his hold on

the throat and wiped his fingers on the fleece. A wound
on his neck was plastered over with a square of adhesive
gauze that was set on in a crooked diamond pattern. He
was restless, working still with the beast, his hands again
on its throat, but he looked up at her suddenly. A kneeling
man, squatting beside a ewe, lifting his hat, a crooked diamond of bloody adhesive plaster on his neck, and she re-
sented the picture and looked toward J.T. for momentary
comfort. The message from the hearth was given, the question asked.

"No quarantine necessary," the man said.

He stood up when he had spoken, and J.T. called his
name: "Mr. Treer, it's John Logan Treer," a slight up-
lifting of a hand. He was tall above the sheep when he
stood up. His hair was burnished in the light when his
hat was off, but dark in a shadow. She was pleased that he
should arise and become beautiful after his ugliness as
seen squatting on the stable floor. He came near to her
and began to talk earnestly of the sheep. She was twisting
her mouth in a faint smiling dissent, her manner saying:
"But I am only a messenger. . . ." He called an order to
the veterinary and walked with her back to the house to
give Drake his report.

———

The flock being purged of disease, J.T. sheared the
adult sheep in May, but the lambs were let keep their

wool and were turned to graze on the fresh new pasture.
The third stable was used for the operation of shearing,
and Walter, at hand, helped in cutting away the fleeces.
The long shears were buried in the dull yellow wool and
a bright, clean felt-like mat, the fleece, rolled back from
the searching blades. Jocelle sat in the sunny doorway
before the labor. They would be making play.

"I see a fleece and I think about Jason."

"I think about Heterogeneosity," Jocelle said.

"Gosh all Jupiter!"

There would be laughter now wherever Jocelle led.
Far out from the house, in the open doorway of the barn,
while the shearing lasted, there was a sensible nonsense
and the upleaping of good bursts of folly. As if she had
run away from Martha's woe, Jocelle kept with the young
men, sharing with them the light labors of the barnyards.
J.T. was known to have a sweetheart somewhere named
Annie Laurie Bond. This young woman, never present,
was continually there in J.T.'s speech and Walter's teasing. In honor of this adored one Jocelle was made to sit
one day on a fine white fleece. Far out from the house,
thus, into the early days of June, to the end of the shearing, mirth and laughter and play. Sometimes she well
knew the west wind carried her voice back to the house
and flung it into fragments, dropped and lost or newly
fluttering, through the old doorways and the darkened
halls.

Her laughter again in the orchard east of the kitchen garden, where the sprays were spread over the trees. Walter would work at the hand pump and J.T. would climb the taller trees or reach the tops with a long nozzle. Well out of the poison spray, Jocelle would sit among the apple boughs, in honor of Annie Laurie, crowned one day with a spray of apple leaves. Logan, the farm agent, would come there.

"Hell is well broke loose in Europe again," fresh news brought by the newcomer.

"Sink your ships without warning."

"War in the North Seas."

"Kitchener went down on the *Hampshire*."

"You wouldn't think they'd dare."

"Kill a general? Whoop!"

Their thoughts played uneasily over the war areas, among the disturbed nations, the disordered histories of peoples. The steady throb of the pump and the fine splash of the spray went forward while the voices of the men were still. Then:

"War. Unformed matter. In it all the seeds of nature."

"A heterogeneous heterogeneosity."

"What?" Logan asking.

"It's in the book of wonders."

"In the book of Dickon's wisdom. . . ."

"The mythical book. Nobody ever saw it."

She would not tell them that she had seen *The Cosmo-*

graph, that she owned a copy, that it was hidden in the lower drawer of her chest among the little round balled spheres of her stockings. It had been given in secret and she did not betray the trust. But she dared paraphrase and laughter.

A three-month-old calf, grazing in the orchard, would come from behind to smell at their fingers. Her breath was of fresh warm milk. There were bees from another farm, from Bob Terry's place, over the south hill, sucking nectar from the white clover underfoot. Logan let the calf suck two of his fingers, and Jocelle tried this also, to feel the soft rough tongue lapping on her skin and pulling at her flesh. Their voices fluttered an argument with the late breezes of June and came faintly to the house, to the bridge, the lookout, and to Martha indoors, where she tended the housekeping or wrote fragments of herself onto fragmentary sheets of paper, rhythmic lines and half-rhymed experience, drawn down into a few hard, tender sayings.

The work of rebuilding the tobacco barn went forward, and the silage tank arose as a tower of concrete beyond the farther stable. Dickon stayed at Wolflick much through the summer and into the autumn. Within the house another argument:

"Hell in Europe."

"Europa, that is. There's a white bull inside the story somewheres. Zeus, Jupiter, got himself changed to a white bull and went to the field where she was out to pick flowers."

Heated arguments would follow, at night on the bridge where the cool night air fell after the setting of the sun. Or beside the evening fire of early autumn:

"There was chaos, unformed matter. Chaos contained all the seeds of nature, of thought, night, Terra, the Universe, love and hate . . ."

"All right, chaos, then."

"A heterogeneous mass. Into it came a breath, Erebus, the spirit that lives in eternal darkness, and the heterogeneosity was put in violent motion. Congenial parts assembled. Matter appeared, and against there was matter appeared attraction, kind for kind."

"Where did kind come from?"

"Kind?"

Tight lips were drawn down over the spoken question. Contempt ran counter to the contemplated explanation. Drake settled back in his chair and looked at his hands where flinty fingernails grew out of soft flesh. Dickon answered, looking sharply upward, his black and white face, weathered and lightly whiskered with a scrubby beard, holding hostile caution.

"Kind was in chaos. All the seeds of nature. I said all. Power in an infinity of degrees. All the active principles of nature: order, figurability, succession, retention. These were there, but they were passive in the upheaval."

"God spake to Noah and said"—Briggs speaking—"God said unto Noah: 'The end of all flesh is come before me; for the earth is filled with violence through them; and, behold, I will destroy them with the earth. Make thee an ark of gopher wood; rooms shalt thou make in the ark, and shalt pitch it within and without with pitch. . . .'"

"Keep still until I get through. Passive in the upheaval, I said."

"Rooms in the ark, I said. Man alive, God made places for the kinds when he made the ark through old Noah. Rooms, it says. A room here and a room there, up and down, like cells in a honeycomb. Ready for the kinds. God said unto Noah: 'The end of all flesh is come before me.' Said: 'The earth is filled with violence . . .'"

"Passive in the upheaval . . ."

"Jocelle!" Drake called.

"I'm here, sir, what is it?"

"One says active and one says passive. Which can I believe?"

"Mankind alive. I tell you it's so, like I say. We are still waiting for the waters to dry and the dove to find a foothold, a resten place for the sole of her foot," Briggs said. "The earth is full of violence. One pulls this way and one pulls another. 'I want' can't get shed of 'I'm bound to.'"

A long monologue would name Terra, vegetative order, succession, figurability, retention, each one defined. Intention and Aptitude begat Providence. Providence married

Measure or Perfection, who was the daughter of Contemplation. Presided over the forming world. Brought the animals into existence. Then Man.

"Wait a minute. Who begat Contemplation? You didn't name a progenitor for Providence's wife's daddy." Drake asking. . . .

Stoner Drake, sitting at the head of his table, served his family with meat. His grizzled hair was thrown upward in long thin locks that stood back from his brow. Sitting thus always in dignity, carving slices of roasted beef for the plates beside his elbow, he seemed paternal, benign, patient, even affectionate. He offered the food quietly, without speech, as if he offered charity, as if he gave in pity for their eager physical hungers. When he had served each one, he took a portion to his own plate and began to eat slowly.

"Betelgeuse will rise at about nine o'clock," he said.

Jocelle was thinking of John Logan Treer, as if he were Betelgeuse, the sound of the name bringing to her thought a fine mythical beast, going wherever it willed. A bright, sunlit open space, dimly seen in this half-attentive vision, reached farther and farther into a long sandy shore. Betelgeuse walked freely through the widely spread light, a strong creature, beautiful in limb, a horse and rider now. The man had grave troubled eyes when he was not laughing, eyes gray shading to green perhaps. She could not remember the color, being absorbed with the gaze and look, swift or slow, toward her or away. He would draw his hat down so that it shaded his eyes and look off toward some far distance. He had sent her a book on the breeding of sheep and he had talked of the Southdowns, their own kind. All the sheep were well now, the old jaundiced ewe having been killed.

"It's clear as a bell tonight," Martha said, and the fine beast, Betelgeuse, became a star again, taking place in its constellation. "I want to see the great nebula in Orion. My field glass."

The young men made soft-spoken rhymes on Martha's further monologue of *beta* and *theta*. She was still speaking:

"I'm of a mind to set up a three-inch glass on the roof of the front porch. You'd look south and keep free of the trees."

"But look how you'd freeze."

"I saw the two of Polaris on a cold night, five below zero. Not here, of course. A magnifying power of a hundred."

"And what did they look like?" Walter asked.

"Like a yellow grain of illuminated salt beside a bluish grain. It was a good night. The air was cut clean toward the north." She dreamed slightly, being for the moment gone far.

111

Walter held two large grains of coarse salt from the salt-dish before the lamp, catching them carefully between his thumb and a finger. Drake spoke then, his speech slow, clear, and loud, as if it were final:

"If you clutter up the roof of my gallery with a three-inch glass, I want results. Spirals and doubles. I want origins and from-whiches. I want toward-whats and mathematicals.

"I can take my spy-glass, the one I use to spy out what Tobin does and to shake up Elkin's laziness. Last night, up on the bridge, I took a long shot at the Galaxy. Cold there, too, and the air was clear. It takes cold to pinch the fog out of the sky. On the bridge, too, you can hear a mighty heap on a still night. See and hear. I heard a car off on the highroad east, and that's above three miles. Some befuddled son-of-the-devil that started from nowhere and he's goen nowhere as fast as a gasoline engine can take him. I heard the roar through the country. To go somewhere, he thinks, God knows! Splutter splutter, blub, blurrrr, hummm. He's all night on his way. Out of his bed. To go nowhere sixty-five miles an hour. The earth turns, how much an hour? Answer me, Walter."

"I don't know, sir."

"God knows, he don't know. How much Marthy?"

"About, say, a thousand miles."

"I hear splutter-blub in a fair way to split open his sides, his little gasoline jackass goen forty-five miles in the hour.

112

Up this way and down that way, and after you think: 'Well, he's gone now,' he's back again in another instance, the same God-forsaken, hurry-up, goen-nowhere, today and forever. Poor fool, poor lame belly-achen, hungry, empty son-of-a-woman, mistook what he wanted firstplace."

"Caught in a fox-trap!" Walter cried out.

"There's the Parcæ, the Fates," Dickon said. "Time—past, present, and future. What's her name, the one that holds the distaff? She's got it in her hand. Then there's Atropos. Means 'No turn back.' Clotho was the name of the other one, Clothy. Branches of cedar will do, Juniper. Turtle doves and black sheep."

"I don't want any of your black sheep. What, Walter, is the best hour of a man's life?"

"The middle hour, I reckon."

"The best hour? What?" J.T. cried out. "What is it? It's the hour he first falls in love and knows she loves him back. That's what I call the climax."

"Which first?" Walter shouted to him over Dickon's account of Lachesis, whose name he had now remembered.

"Allotment," Dickon cried out. "Cut here, she says, and the last one snips it off with the scissors."

Stoner Drake sat at the east side of the room. The board reached dimly forward from his hands that rested quietly at the sides of his plate. His teeth, although neglected, being finely made, shone, flashing in and out as he spoke in high feeling, and they were momentarily forgiven their broken lines and their stains. Next to him on his right Walter sat, his nephew, large, careless of his posture, smoking his cigarette even while he ate his food. He would run an index finger into his short, stubby, close-clipped hair and press upward with his finger at his heavy full lips. J.T. sat next, Drake's grandson, like Jocelle in general appearance—the light brown hair and dark gray eyes shading to violet. He was earnest of what he said, and his vague abstraction gave seriousness to the haphazard conversation of the board, as if he stated the cause of their being assembled here and reached in his person the trodden ground outside, the running fields, the sheep, the broken woodlands, the outlying farms and the lanes that went toward the towns, the mills, the mending shops, and the markets with the people coming and going. Dickon was at the end of the board, opposite the host. His blue cotton shirt was buttoned at the throat with a white china button. His clothes were drab and sun-faded but they were neatly kept. His face was long and haunted, thin and strong. The uneven stubble of his beard, which was of a three or four days' growth, laid shadows lightly over his cheeks. His knife and fork seemed too small for his large square hands. When he had finished eating, he filled a pipe and lit it, throwing the burnt match across toward the fireplace with a stiff, angular gesture of his left arm. Jocelle, who sat next to him on his right, leaned toward

Martha. She seldom looked toward Dickon. J.T. said that
he was a good carpenter and excellent builder. She liked
the fine, clean silage tank he had constructed and she
granted him carpentry, but she gave him nothing more.
She looked toward J.T. and Walter, whose faces would
light with attention if she spoke and who had associations
with Logan and knew a part of what he knew. J.T. spoke
to her sometimes across the board, some comment unrelated to the passing discussion, and it was as if he whispered
a confidence or passed her opinion to the absent Logan
and linked her to their common thought.

But J.T. looked up now suddenly, looking toward the
head of the board and speaking directly to his grandfa-
ther·

"What would you do if the house should catch fire?
House burn down?"

"What would we do?" Several asked it, Martha speaking beneath Walter's derisive laugh. "Oh, what would
we do?"

Silence followed. Jocelle bent to her plate and ate the
last of her bread. Martha scraped lightly at her plate with
a fork, making scarcely a sound. Drake put food slowly
into his mouth. His face was set and his thin lips bent to
meet the food. J.T. arose from his seat and walked away
from the room. Walter went, calling J.T. a fool in the
hall. Dickon went toward the kitchen and later he crossed
the dog-run to sit with Tobin by the cabin fire. Martha

had left the table suddenly, but she lingered, seeming careless in the careful folding of her napkin. She went quickly when this was done. Jocelle called Nettie Tobin to carry away the plates, and later she cleared the napkins from the board and thrust them into a drawer of the sideboard. Drake spoke slowly: "If the house burns . . ."

"What'll he do if the house burns down? Who asked it? Walter? He's a scared little she-boy, weighs near two hundred. It wasn't Walter though. John Thomas it was. John Thomas Drake asks a question. What'll he do when the house burns down? That is to say, I. What'll he do when the whole world is drowned in a lake of fire. Query: What'll he do? He didn't stay to smoke his cigarettes. And Marthy went. Marthy is a good girl. Takes a very good edication, edgication, education. How's your corporosity sagaciating? We used to ask it on the street. 'Good morning, how's your corporosity today?' Jocelle, then, the daughter of a slut named Catharine, a big-breasted woman that cuckolded my boy Ben and sent him to his grave. Jocelle, I wouldn't even know for sure she's Ben's brat but she looks mightily like the Drake people, blond like John Thomas they call J.T., but otherwise like Marthy . . . but a bigger frame." He called her to him.

"Come here, Jocelle. Firstplace I want to ask you a question."

"Yes, sir."

"Pour me out a glass from the squat jug."

She poured the sweet wine, three-fourths of a glass, as he wanted it.

"Jocelle, he says: 'What if the house burns?' What, Jocelle, is fire?"

"Fire? . . . I don't know, sir."

"Find out, then."

She opened a large dictionary on a table in the rear of the room and fluttered the pages, to read presently:

"Fire—noun, Old English, *fir* . . . Greek, *pur,* Latin, *purus,* pure . . . compare Empyrean, also pyre.

"First definition: The evolution of light and heat in the combustion of bodies; combustion; state of ignition. . . . Here's a note: Anciently *fire,* air, earth, and water were regarded as the four elements of which all things were composed.

"Second definition: Fuel in a state of combustion, as on a hearth or in a stove or a furnace. Third definition: The burning of a house or town; a conflagration."

"That's enough. What, Jocelle, do you make out of it? Remember out of it? What's fire?"

"Old English, *fir,* Greek, *pur,* Latin, *purus,* English, *pure.* Empyrean, Pyre, Funeral Pyre. Evolution of light and heat in combustion. On a hearth, in a stove, in a furnace. The burning of a house or a town: a conflagration. Then here's fire-blast, fire-brick . . . fire-brigade . . . fire-dog . . . fire-fly . . . fire-hose . . . fire-insurance. . . ."

117

"And what's that, the last one?"

"Insurance against loss by fire."

"Is there any insurance against the general conflagration? Against Empyrean? Pyre?"

"I don't know. They tell me so, told me so. . . . Yes, told me the Redeemer . . . Told me Jesus . . ."

"I don't say it again. I said it once and for all. Put the decanter back and set away the squat jug in the lower cupboard. There's a mort of unnecessary pain. There's a life principle. A good woman lives by it, lives up to it. No slut, a woman, hearty and kind, loved one man and clave to him. If God would but talk plain to mankind, say fact, quit mystery. . . .

"I went out on the bridge last night, near one o'clock, Jocelle, no new thing to do. Pollux off in the east. Cassiopeia over the Pole, and the Milky Way gone down, set. You know, Jocelle, I named you. Born, you were, in the room across the way, my room now. Then Ben died and it was almost as much as a man could bear to know how his life was broke, how they had married him to a trull and he tried to hold it up and make nature out of it. Then Catharine goes off, leaving her child the way you'd think she was less than a dog-bitch, old Minnie in the back yard that wouldn't leave her pups to hunt till they got weaned. Shut to the cupboard door, there, and turn the key.

"Empyrean. The light of the upper world, the fire of heaven, the blinding light of the sky. It's said the Ameri-

can eagle can look at the sun. I knew a man once was blind
from the snow. Eyes then. Eyes are the receptacle of light,
the mirror of fire, the opposite, the complement, the
toward-what. Two little suns in the head of a man made
to take in the light of the sun and to turn it into sense.
What would the eyes be without light?"

"Like a mole, maybe."

"Jocelle, what's the war? What's this war?"

"I'm not sure I know."

"Find out."

"Yes, sir."

"They make war now with gas. Greek fire brought down
to date. Conflagration. . . . Tear gas for the eyes. Fetch
the Book there, the Bible. I knew a man once was blind
from the snow. Open the Book near the end.

" 'These things saith he which hath the sharp sword
with two edges: I know . . . where thou dwellest, even
where Satan's seat is. . . . He that hath an ear, let him
hear what the Spirit saith.' . . . Sardis . . . Smyrna . . .
Pergamos . . . Laodicea. Places speak and are spoken to.
Famine, then, he says. Judgment from above on the Earth.
'The first angel sounded, and there followed hail and fire
mingled with blood.' . . . The first woe is past: I've read
it through time and time again. How can a man untangle
this mystery?

"His lake of fire. Jocelle, where's Walter gone?"

"I think he went to his room, sir."

119

"His room?"

"J.T. went to the stable to close in the sheep."

"He takes very good heed of the eow-bitches. Let him hang the key on the nail beside the chimney. Jocelle, read once again the definition. Turn back to the beginning. Read again. . . ."

Later in the night Martha came back to the fireplace and carefully covered the flames with dead ashes. All were now gone to rest. Above in her room Jocelle heard the scraping of the shovel when the fire in the parlor was covered. The kitchen fire was tended likewise.

Night after night Martha performed this last midnight task. Each fire was visited and each was carefully guarded with dead ashes, each carefully scraped together and covered. The young men called her Curfew then. "Here comes Curfew," a whisper went down through the hall, or the male voice broke over the word, "Curfew."

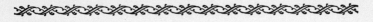

V

MARTHA walked out into the sunshine of a mild February day and sat to rest on a bench before the stables. Walter and J.T. were taking the sheep with their lambs across the beaten turf before the stables to graze them on the pasture grass of the west field. The high baaing of the ewes stood as a deep running tone behind the thin short bleats of the lambs, and the whole receded suddenly as the beasts spread over the green hillside. Jocelle had come to sit beside Martha, and the sheep being pastured for the day, the young men gathered about Martha's seat, Logan having come. They were looking at the stables as if they had not seen them before.

"Horse sense is all over this place," J.T. said. "Left, by God, when old Firebrand first kept stud here."

"The water-tank and the way it is disposed," Logan replied, approving.

To the east beyond the stretch of lawn the house stood against the dun and black masses of high trees, clearly shaped now in side elevation—the large building, the bridge, the lower mass of the cabin with the lookout above Now several pigeons, like seagulls, walked on the railing of the bridge. Near at hand the three openings in the three stables let the sunlight in among brown shadows. Within the middle doorway water ran from a pipe into a concrete tank.

"The water-tank, yes," J.T. said. A discourse followed as he brought the past to hand in one way or another It was thus then, and so and so could happen. One after another added to the undisputed argument. The great-grandfather, father of the old Jocelle, has got the fields out of the timberland. He had fought the trees. The battle of Tippecanoe stood also among his battles. "Placed the house," J.T. said, "just where it ought to be."

"Scratched with a horse-hair on the rump of old times."

"Horse sense built the stables firstplace."

The work of the mid-morning done, Stoner Drake sat withindoors, asleep in his chair by the slow fire. The horn hung over the chair-post at his left shoulder. Logan would be talking in long bursts of protest, scarcely caring whether he made his argument clear or obscure, assuming agreement. Walter was divided from the argument by his apathetic inattention, for he had no bond with these fields, having no Ainsley blood in him.

"And built good stables, horse sense did."

"Then Alex-smartness smote . . ."

"Smote the rock of credit, I reckon."

"Alex-smartness smote the rock of family credit and underground springs of revenue turned back to the source."

"Dried up is what you mean."

"It wasn't Alex-smartness, neither," Logan said. He pulled his hat forward on his head as if he made ready for a fight. His eyes began to sparkle and snap their fire. He became ten years older on the instant and was no longer a boy with a theory but a man now with a conviction. "It was two things or, at most, three. Horse-power is now manufactured at Detroit. That's one. Very well, let the horse go. Cattle and sheep, then, and grain and tobacco. System comes in, point two. Streams of revenue go out but mighty few ever come in, mighty little trickles back. Buys high and sells cheap. They've made him a beggar. Doles he'll be given next, loans so he can buy more. Point three is his own blasted, God-forsaken inaction, non-action, let-it-alone, and the manufacturers got him by the throat fifty years ago."

"Old Firebrand couldn't compete with Detroit," Walter said.

"Let old Firebrand go then. I'm talken about the present."

They were all talking, speech upon speech. Martha defended Detroit for a moment and said she wished that she had a filly out of one of the high-class stables there.

"What are we talken about?" J.T. cried out.

"About enough . . . and a-plenty. Before another decade we'll have a new man," Logan answered him.

"It takes a war to get a living for the peasant."

"Sixty-six to sixteen. Fifty years of Lincolnmania. The worship of the cabin-man. The cult of Jesus grew parallel with the growth of empire. Merged then . . ."

"I don't like your talk," Martha said. "Cult of Jesus."

J.T. turned upon her. "It's God's own truth. You can't deny the shrines, temples, banks, cars, townhalls, schools, streets, hospitals, counties, cities, shafts, parks."

"It's the tendency to centralize. The mind loves a unit, wants a unit. Wants to bring everything to focus. A habit derived from the habit of the eyes. Focus. Looks back upon itself and sees the machinery, itself, focus. Thinks everything outside is subject to focus. Begs focus. Borrows focus. Gets focused."

"While everybody looks at the pigeon fly out of the hat."

"Exactly."

"Under cover of the popular religion the Barons of the Big Fortunes grew. Learned how to sell things to the government. How t', how t', how t'."

Martha and Logan were the speakers.

"Builds another Lincoln gee-gaw."

"Lost the man under the myth."

"Sop to the common dog-man."

"Cult of the log cabin, when did it start? About the time of Andrew Jackson?"

"Every man born west of the Appalachians in 1809 was born in a cabin. The green-timber age was gone by 1850 or so."

"The barons loved the cabin-man. Sold him goods, transportation, oil. Taught him how to sing 'Yankee Doodle' too. And got his vote. Rolled around old cabins on wheels in election campaigns."

Walter began to sing to break the swift dialogue:

"Mounted to the cabin with his orders in his hand . . .
Said the two locomotives are a-goen to bump!
Said mounted to the cabin with his orders in his hand."

Martha was thin and of transparent pallor, sitting in the sun. Her small thin hands locked themselves in and out as she talked. She sat on the bench the hostlers had used when there were colts to be trained and groomed. She looked up sidewise toward Logan while Walter sang, as if the song weighted the argument. She seemed to be aging although she was but thirty-six. Her brown hair was lightly scattered with flying threads of white that spread as an untamed spray, that drifted unwanted and unassimilated to the brown mass. Her hair was cut to hang in locks about her ears, a piquant dressing, over which blew the few vagrant and stiff, frizzled, uncurled threads, as a scanty frost. In the sunlight she disregarded the gray and dressed herself to the soft brown mass, but at midnight indoors she would tend all the fires as if she were a grandame or a witch. J.T. stood above her, tall and thin. He wanted to be about his own business, to be raising fine cattle on Drake's acres, to be marrying somewhere, but the threatened war kept him in a state of unrest. His work clothes were stained from his early morning labors—grease from the gasoline engine he had adjusted and mud from the cowpens. He stood above Martha pulling restlessly at his knuckles.

"It's my belief we'll have a new man. Before another decade He'll begin," Logan said.

"And what man will he be?" Questions plying from three quarters.

"Simple enough. The upstanding, intelligent man. No bathos. No tears. We won't know where he was born. We'll know him for what he thinks. No man of sorrows. A man of sound sense. He'll stand up in his world. Old sculpture *pathétique* can go! Loose-jointed *ecce homo!* One protoplasm is like another protoplasm, and why all the stir about the birth? Life is what we want. Where's the life of the man? we'll ask."

"And when will that be, sir?"

"When Europe gets through fighting."

"That's hit, that's hit. When she gets through!"

"We'll have a new man. Good sense and a just peace. No blubber. Able to pool his interests with his neighbor's. The co-operative man."

"He's a smoke dream, your new man," J.T. said. "I don't see the fellow. Try to get one and you'll get an engine. He'll always go down. The mob-man wins. Goes where he's told in the end. Wants a full paunch. While he's got it or thinks he's got it, all right. Turn around three times and do a somersault and kiss yourself on the way back. Goes down, your man does, in the vapor of his own thought."

Logan stood before Martha and he looked down upon her tenderly, saying:

"Whoop! He's come around to't by the back way. What else but vapor? What we want is good vapor. Acts according to the rules of all vapor. All right. We are such stuff as dreams are made on. The good dream . . ."

He was sorry the moment he had spoken and he ceased to speak too abruptly, letting his distress be known. Regret burned pain into his face, but Martha was alert, she being the one present whose little life seemed more nearly rounded to its sleep. Slowly speaking:

"The hand that wrote that dandled baby Hamlet, I reckon, and kissed hands with Ben Jonson . . . said furtive rosaries, perhaps, and at last knuckled down to death's handshake, the vapor wanting to thaw and dissolve itself into dew. What's dew? Put under ground at Stratford and crying out a dare by the way of some rude country cousin poet, and cursed be he that moves those bones . . ."

"The mob-man again, God's own sake. Country Cousin

knew they'd be moved when they became fashionable
again."

"Get a hundred thousand of him together and he'll hang
anybody, steal, plunder, tear down . . ."

"More about your New Man. Make his case plain,
will y'?"

"He could take three forms." Three fingers were slowly
bent down, one at a time, under the leverage of a thumb.
Jocelle watched the fingers play in the air and she saw
that they were not inflexible matter, that they were bent
with grace as if the three causes, being men, danced a
slow argument behind the curves of bent muscles and
shapely bones. Before the third man was fully developed,
the whole discourse broke into laughter, into some unrelated laughter that followed J.T.'s laughed objection.
The fingers were bent into a hard fist then and laid against
a hip. Logan let arguments be and looked down brightly
musing, his eyes not seeing the sandy beaten floor of the
paddock on which he gazed, his head wavering uncertainly
from side to side, and he had then the sinuous life of a
snake in him. Jocelle saw that if she spoke the men listened
attentively, smiling, without interruption, but that beyond the smile they did not answer her arguments, that
they attended to her person rather than to her opinion,
and that her shapely body and tapering ankle spoke for
her. Logan made a light winding motion toward her with
his hand, as if he would wind her up with meaningful

nonsense. She ceased to speak audibly and looked toward Martha as for guidance.

Walter walked up and down in the bright sun. He would put both hands into his jacket pockets and kick his boots against the post that held the smaller bench. His frame was like that of his uncle, old Drake, but larger. He would predict war for America. "It's bound to come," he said. "The German submarine policy has already . . ." He would smoke quietly, holding the cigarette far from him while he blew the smoke, as if he did not in fact smoke it. "If it comes," he said, "I'll go, I'll enlist . . ."

"Man, it'll be by the way of a draft."

"I'll not wait for any draft. I want to get the thing over. I want to get my part done so's I can turn my mind to something. By God! I'll say. Let me get at the thing! Show me something to fight, and, by God! I'll blow a hole straight through the blasted tricky, God-darned what-you-may-call-it. Even say we're out so far. . . . Everybody state what he's fighting for might get a showdown. But it'll be to protect American bizness wherever she floats a flag. Bizness as usual. Food blockade . . . Munition blockade. God, it's a puken age. I want to be something in my own name."

Jocelle looked at him, wondering what he would be if he had his entire will. He wanted to move through some medium that was fixed, himself being free. She did not know what way of life he desired, or what profession or trade he might claim, and his crying out thus made of him a sort of mystery as if he assumed importance from his angry demand. Not knowing how to fix him among the professions, she let him sink back into the mass of all the young men of the country, for he had cried out for them. Three now were standing together before the long bench where she and Martha sat. With Martha they seemed to have something or to share something, some matter which it was hers to know indirectly. She had been put apart, as being aside from their discussions, their plans to re-create the world in vapors, in meanings and sense. It was the war, she thought, that made the difference between them. They knew more of it. She resolved deeply within to know the war as they would know, to be equal with them or better in knowing. Determination quickened her heart for the instant and drew a sensation of tight chords within her neck. She would know all. They were speaking further:

"Take the farm I sold, my patrimony . . ."

His patrimony, a farm six miles away on the road to Anneville, stood to the fore to make a point. "If Gibson ever pays out in five years, it'll take a war to underwrite the bill. . . ." She understood these instances as well as they. Logan had sold his patrimonial farm to devote himself entirely to his profession. It was a little farm six miles southeast of Wolflick. Or J.T. had an example to offer:

"Take Bob Terry across the hill yonder."

Wreaths and carefully made spirals of smoke floated

toward her. She asked suddenly, being excluded from their conjectures:

"What is the best part of a man?"

"Best according to what?"

"The best, the most lasty. What is it?"

They looked at the ground, asking themselves, each in his own way. Martha pulled at her scarf and smiled, subtracting the query from sense. Walter scratched at the bridge of his nose with a fingernail. "Why would there be any best?" he asked. J.T. spoke almost at once: "The soul, I reckon, whatever it is." In the quiet that followed this speech, Logan and Walter looked at her with amiable surprise. Then Logan began to talk around her inquiry and he brought it back to his theory, being gay over his definitions, as if he did not value the statement of them now, at this moment. Smiling upon her, he made long sentences without beginning or end, and he leaned slightly forward with a stress that asked: "Am I not right?" saying:

"The all, all-which and all-what, together everything and whatever, all the functions in one. Finally it would be the part that felt the we-ness of the race."

Walter cried out suddenly, his eyes earnest and angry. "Talk! talk! talk! Talk forever! It would be the man, what he *is*. It would be Himself. He. He, him, and go-to-hell any other. It would be God-knows. God's own two-legged son-of-a-b with his shirt-tail out or in, whichever he damn pleases."

131

Walter's opinion was let stand foremost then, unaltered. He walked back toward the front of the stable and looked uneasily at Logan, as if he distrusted argument and violence for the ends to which they might lead. J.T. began to speak slowly after a little, looking away from Walter's flushed face. He sank to a squatting position, resting the weight of his body upon a thigh pressed against a shank and heel. Chewing at a twig, he spoke:

"Say we could come to the state of mind we'll have five years, eight years, ten, from now. 'The war,' we'll say, 'was all bunk. . . . The war was big business. . . .' But meanwhile it's got to get us over the years."

"Oh, the war," Martha cried out in Walter's anger, her anger at his outburst directed now away from him. And laughing then: "I didn't raise my eyes to look at soldiers."

"You'll likely raise them to look at a million. Ten hundred thousand brown men, khaki-men. Dressed out to eat your own bully beef and your own wheat. Smoke your own bright burley," Logan answered her.

He was speaking of her grandfather's bright burley tobacco, grown to the peal of his sharp bell or the thrust of his stiff horn. It was for the most part housed in the barn, the newly built structure, where it was graded and piled neatly on wagon frames to be hauled soon to the market. Some had already been sold. It was their chief money crop, that she well knew. Martha lifted her head to speak suddenly, asking:

"How could you get a changed man, a new man, unless his way of livelihood were changed? His religion changed, but most of all, his occupation, his way of making his living?"

Logan looked at her earnestly, frowning, considering her point. The sun shone aslant across his face and lit his forehead. For the moment the light on his hair was gold, but he pulled his hat forward, and his mouth became a thin, tight line. "He might change it," he said, gripping his fist in a half-open palm, beating his hands together. "He might have to change."

"Mob-man would make 'im?"

"Oh, God have pity on us!" Martha cried out.

They stood together without speaking, staring from one another to the sandy floor or the encircled hills. They were off again in discourse: Comity of nations. An over-lord, a power to guide us. . . . We used to call it balance of power. . . . Balance of Power is right! All the balance and then some. . . . A fat man with a roll of jelly for a belly, an old soak. . . .

Jocelle did not speak to them then, loving all of them in quiet. Logan and Walter had taken off their leather jackets and they trailed them under an arm. Logan's leather vest was pulled open. He would shake his head now, his hat off, tossing back long imaginary locks. He seemed to be riding a cantering animal, making laughter with Martha. Out of his centaur mouth gracious words

133

were flowing. He was riding, unshod, on swift horse limbs, little feet, thin shanks, strong thighs, his hair thrown up in a wind. He was standing, feet drawn together, Chiron, the good centaur, chanting a line, standing before Martha who was slowly dying, a lovely girl, the sun bright now on her dark hair and his rippling mouth:

> "Give me a spark of Nature's fire,
>   That's all the learning I desire;
>   And tho' I drudge thro' dub and mire
>   At pleugh . . . plough . . . plow . . ."

"What's dub?"

"Dub's Scotch. Scotch for water-hole. Drudge through a Kentucky water-hole, by George!"

"What George?"

"The Father of the Country, by Hec!"

"What Hec?"

She heard their sounds, laughing with their laughter. They, what were they saying? They took no account of the blasting horn, the bridge, the beaked prow of the house. Bright water churned over high ocean stones and lay out laterally rising and falling, a bright flow, a tide, themselves out in the dimpling sea, themselves here in the sun before the stables.

"Food blockade: the Germans have eaten all the dogs."

"How did we come to this place?"

"Ask History."

"Ask anybody."

Their speech ran forward with sense, ran ahead of sense, playing backward to another sense in laughter. "Did it matter who slept sleep with the woman?" Walter then speaking. A long picture-drama built about a no-man's care who slept sleep in Kit's bed or Dell's. "A lousy play." J.T. brought the jack stallion from the stable and tied it outside in the bright sun. They were laughing toward her now, and she smiled them away from all theories. Her hands were warm in the sun and ruddy in the reflected glow of Martha's red scarf. Care called her to the kitchen, where Nettie Tobin was preparing a dinner of roast lamb and whatever greens she herself might suggest, but she had suggested none. The large front pasture rolled away toward the south before the house, and over it were scattered here and there a few ancient trees, some of them blighted by disease or lightning. At the farther end of this pasture the land rose to the highroad that lay behind the tall hedge growth. While she did not attend to their voices, they were back again at their opinions.

"I want to get the thing done," Walter cried out. "Why wasn't I born ten years earlier, twenty, then. Comes up to manhood and meets this thing, War, right in his blasted face. All the time, when he was a boy, he thought that when he got grown, turned twenty-one or twenty-five, he'd do this thing or that or the other. Trained in school. It's time now to begin to be. And here's three years, war, four, any number you damn say, in ahead, before anything he's got in mind."

"You're right enough. Nobody disputes y'."

"What I want is to get the thing over. Want to be something for myself. Can't remember sometimes who I am or what was't I had in mind. God! they're slow, the whole damned lot of 'em is a slow lot of bitches. I want life. Action. A chance to be myself. Show me something to hit and I'll drive a blasted hole straight through, hindsides and fore. God! they're slow. Feel sometimes like I could pitch damnation into the whole war front."

Passing from the county seat toward the north, going here and there by the ill-tended byways, Logan would stop at Wolflick to linger in the stable for a half-hour with J.T. He would call at Drake's fireside, where polite interchanges would follow, or he would walk with Martha to the parlor. Leaving, he would linger with Jocelle on the portico and make grave gests. Had she plowed for corn? Had she sowed the clover seed? There were reports of the town—the prices of foodstuffs, the dances in Anneville, the knitting girls, the turkey-trot.

"The war, what will it be?"

"You'll find out. It's on our doorsteps already."

"Armies are in the shrubbery."

His farewell: "Corn, the most important crop in American cultivation . . ." The beginning of a speech to be delivered that day at the Pleasant Hill schoolhouse. With a platform gesture he would be gone.

Martha coughed frequently and was often ill. With Jocelle she clipped from the newspapers matter that related to the war and pasted the clippings into a scrapbook, as if the war were over, as if it were history. "It'll end before the summer," she said. "The American gesture will forbid it."

Among the fields of Wolflick the men made ready for corn, the maize, that had been called in eloquence the most important crop in American cultivation. The fields were plowed in April while the larks and the quail cried out musical notes from the overturned turf. After each day's plowing the harrow was sent across the cloddy area, and later the whole was harrowed again. J.T. selected the ears for seed and Jocelle carried an armful of them to Stoner Drake. She murmured timidly of the test-box and how it might be made, and of the sure method of detecting the unfertile seed. Drake took from his pocket a sharp knife and cut off the tip of each grain he examined, looking closely at the germ revealed.

"It's good enough seed corn," he said.

She gathered up the ears and went on tiptoe from the

room, Drake still in contemplation as he held the grains
of corn in his hand, as he stared at the stippled surface
of the mantel uprights, where the old paint was cracked
in fantastic traceries. Leaving his gaze thus fixed, she went
softly out. Her own looks went freely with the bright sun
on the intense green of the grass, on the cold blossoms of
the tulips along the borders, where the smooth stones led
away from the house door through the small white gate
and toward the stables among the blown feathers of the
hens, and on the soft brown coat of the new-born calf.
The chill of the spring sent shivers of delight through her
skin. The seed corn was tumbled back into the barrel beside the corn-sheller and covered carefully with an old
sack. Two large dark horns from the head of a Jersey bull
had been fixed on the corridor wall of the stable, and over
the horns the bridles and halters were often hung. A
proud chicken cock walked out of the shed, to be clear of
the shade of the wall. Out in the sun his comb quivered
red, and his beak was suddenly the clear yellow of ivory,
his body and his tail coverts gleaming with the fire that
suddenly shone as reflected from his tossing plumes. He
went gingerly out from the cool shadow into the bright
sunlight, as if he walked lightly, fearing to be overtaken
by the necessities of food. In the sunlight he hopped del-
icately from the ground to a sloping pole and went daintily
over a tall fence, Logan with him in the slow free lift of
his proud feather. Jocelle laughed at his excess of caution

and, being without plan or caution, being yielded to the slow, cool spring, she took a bridle from the bull's horns and saddled a horse, a little brown mare, and rode away toward the south through the front driveway. Logan would be speaking to her, whether present or absent, whether she were walking beside him or riding alone on the mare, stepping off thus on the four limbs of the mare in a swinging, running walk. At hand in fact, he would be speaking to Drake.

"It's only in times of great waste that farmstuffs bring prices fit to yield the farmer a living." His hand, crumpled to a fist, would strike the arm of his chair as he spoke.

"You think, then, we'll make a liven while the war lasts?" Drake asked. There would be amiable agreements here, for Logan had put the flock of sheep in a state of health.

Amiable agreements up the stairs and down the long hall to the bridge and out into the open, under the bright sun, to sit there on the bench overlooking the barnyards and the near-lying fields. A great blast on the horn to bring Tobin, with questions and answers flowing back and forth from the bridge to the barnyard, and a tolerant smile played as if in dissimulation around the thin mouth.

"Oh, yes, while the war lasts."

"What remedy have you got for't, young man?"

Meeting her beside the clock, her grandfather said to her: "You didn't come when I called you on the horn."

She had not heard the blast; she had been walking in the front pasture with Logan. She stood momentarily fearful beside his chair and waited until he spoke again, and then he told his wish without anger, anger put by. The duty performed, she sewed the breadths of cloth to make herself a dress, to be ready for the summer. Skirts would be short, Martha said, and boots would be high, well to the top of the calf of the leg. Leather was never more scarce and never were boots so prodigal of it.

"Mob-men, I reckon," Jocelle said.

"Goes where he's herded."

"The men will never go out of America."

"A new government in Russia. They'll drop out one by one."

Walter had enlisted with the marines.

"Five million men we could send over," Martha said.

Jocelle saw five million men, the blades of grass in the front pasture assisting her. The grass walked, four after four, in a neat order, going somewhere or coming there. They were trampling down the earth and beating the hills out of line. They were walking upon Wolflick, swarming over the south hill-rim and trampling the trees. They brought fire and terror, destruction, their path being a path of devastation. Walter and J.T. and John Logan Treer were with them and were at the same time her only defense against them. They were being trampled under the treading of the grass. She was fleeing out toward the

140

fields, toward the north to hide somewhere in the creek gullies among the shelving rocks, but there was no security. She bent to her seam and murmured as she tried to dispel the too clear picture: "Five million is too many."

Briggs had come with the spring. He cut a great pile of wood beyond the cabin, and the strong thrust of his ax chopped and thumped against the outer walls or entered the opened windows at mid-day. He had felled a tree by the creek and had brought the logs to the calf pen on a drag-slide which two mules conveyed. Before coming he had shaved away his beard and now revealed a large, plump, reddened face, on which a constant paralytic smile played at the left of the mouth. Indoors, resting from his labor, his bare feet patted the kitchen floor with a heavy tread. When Jocelle stood with Drake on the lookout, the ax that plied below would be stilled. Briggs would stand then with his head lowered, holding his hat in his hand.

Drake scarcely noticed the cutting of the wood. Briggs would linger in the kitchen, never offering to enter the diningroom until he was asked there. If he were forgotten, he took his food by the kitchen fire.

"Bid Johnnie Briggs come on," Drake would say. A plate and a cup would be brought to the board. The large flat feet, shod now, would come through the entry. Jocelle would pour a cup of the hot black coffee.

"Let us pray," then, Briggs standing on the floor, not far from the kitchen door. A loud grace, half sung, brief, and ceremonial. "While the earth remaineth, seedtime and harvest, and cold and heat, and summer and winter, and day and night shall not cease. . . . Every moving thing that liveth shall be meat for you. . . ."

Jocelle would set the cup of coffee beside the plate, this her amen to what had been said.

"Eat your dinner," Drake would say.

"Thanks, kind sir, thank y'."

"Why did you shave off your face?" Drake asked him. "Didn't your beard grow in pretty deep?"

"I shaved it, sir, for a fancy. It was known to me that hair on a face is not pleasant to some."

"How long have you been covered?"

"A matter of nine years."

Playing Mozart to please Martha, who lay resting above, Jocelle would hear the two short blasts followed by one long one, and she would go quickly toward the sound. Later she would be running through the upper pasture or riding far back into the largest field. She would be carrying letters to the mailbox at the roadside gate. She would be bringing papers from a cupboard. All day the strong blows of the ax would thrust at the wood. She was tall and slight, running bent forward, her body bowed to thrust forward from the thrust of her long, round limbs. Her pale brown hair would be bound back with a fillet of

142

bright ribbon. She slipped about lightly through these
sounds—the ax, the calling foxhorn, the admonitions that
came from the fireside or from the bridge, from the couch
above stairs. Carrying orders, carrying cries, plans, con-
demnations, she went lightly about.

A sick old hound breathed heavily by the cool summer
hearth. Loud reports of footsteps came from the upper
hall, silence following. Briggs was at the kitchen fire drying his large, strong feet after he had bathed them. They
were burned a deep pink by the sun and were rich with
blood. His smile came as he looked upward at Jocelle who
was passing, and she was aware of his large eyes, his strange
mouth, his unearthly laughter, his shaven face.

Later, in the diningroom, while Jocelle arranged the
board for the noon meal, he came slowly through the
doorway. He had never before come through the door
unless he had been invited by the master of the house.
His hat was held limply at his side. His clothes were
dusted with the powdered bark of the wood he had been
cutting. His eyes, that had been lowered, were lifted now
to look at her. His face was bright with his perpetual
smile, and his breath was quick in excitement. He was
speaking, and she felt herself debased by what he was
saying. He followed her to the farther side of the table
and stood near her when she turned suddenly.

"I shaved it off to please you. I heard it said hair is not
pleasant to a young girl."

He lifted his hands and made a slight motion as if he were about to raise them for prayer, but they veered and waved lightly about, sweeping toward himself as if they gathered something to his bosom. "To please you," he said. She stared at him, scarcely hearing his bleak gallantry. "I did it to please you and nobody else," he whispered.

She stepped back three steps toward the hall door. "You didn't do it to please me," she said in anger. "Don't make jokes with me."

He went away. He cut no more at the woodpile he had brought to the calf pen. In the kitchen he sat through the noon hour and later he took a few crusts of bread and a little meat and went out.

"Did Johnnie Briggs go away?" Drake asked.

Nobody had seen him go beyond the kitchen door. He did not come in at nightfall.

———

J.T. hung a large flag from the upper rail of the porch to hang broadside below the upper floor. "Still my country," he said as he walked away, to justify his act, and: "Hurrah for Stephen Decatur!" Thus he had chosen his way and his belief. He had news of Walter, whose training went rapidly forward. "What whim is this?" Drake called out. "Walter a gay cavalier." They retold their responses to the news of the enlistment.

144

"He's about right," J.T. said.

"Wants a frolic. Cavalerio Drake."

"He'll never go out of America."

"He'll be among the first to go. In the marines."

"What's it all about?"

"I'll tell y'. Matter enough. Save Belgium. Comity of nations. Save France. War to bring peace. War to end all wars." The long discourses flowed over the board, over the parlor, over the portico. Two letters came from Walter. Jocelle and Martha began to knit, joining the knitting women. Yarns were sent from Anneville. The needles seemed stiff in hand. Jocelle wove the long strands of yarn, a little stitch thrown through another to make a mesh, the work done slowly. She had seen a brown uniform on the streets in the town, and again she had seen a train-load of such brown men passing through Lester, their heads and arms leaning from the windows of the cars. "The American gesture," Martha said, when she was told of these appearances.

Logan came in from the outlying farms, roughly dressed in brown, the cheapest he could buy, for the prices had gone higher. He rode over miles of rough turnpike. He told Jocelle of his family, his upbringing, of the small farm where his mother and father had lived and died. He would take her to drive outward over the hill, along the stretch of sandy creek-road and thence by the rough ill-tended county byway to the main road, the compact highway. Back again, he would have told her of his theory of human relations, of capital, of wealth stored and in flux, of leadership, of communal interchanges. He was writing his theory of farm-redress and he brought his manuscripts to her for safekeeping as they were finished. Giving them to her, he had kissed her gravely, and had stood then with his hand on her throat as if he made some secret compact with her after he had spoken freely.

There would be discussion again in the parlor or in the sunny portico, in the open space before the stables. The war, a war, any war, this war, causes, ends, finals, guilt, necessity, probability, guesses, reasonings, conclusions—these were endlessly pursued. The young men were continually waiting, scarcely able to undertake any enterprise that required more than the oncoming days. At evening the morning papers were searched again under the lamp.

"Walter's way may have been best," Logan said. "Ran out to meet the blasted thing."

"It's in him to go meet it, whatever 'tis. All is, I wish I could call a year my own now."

They would keep Logan at his work, J.T. said to Jocelle. Standing before the portico, dropping the newspaper sheets he had read: "He'll be teaching the farms . . ." Out in the drive, walking with Logan, or with him in Martha's room above, to chat there with the ailing woman, there would be talk of better farming, of war, of heavy

146

yields, of the terracing of hillsides toward the east of the
county, where the steep hills had induced the washing
of plowed fields. North, he said, the farmers were beginning to use more milk cattle. Dairy farms, grasslands, and
the soil would build up steadily. Logan gone, the soil elements were delineated gayly with Martha, or read from
the journals—water, carbon, silica, aluminum, iron, mag-
nesia, soda, sulphuric acid, nitrogen, phosphoric acid, pot-
ash, lime; to restore the fertility of soil, restore the three
elusive elements.

"Oh, listen, the chickadee! He eats daily from two hundred to five hundred insects, or eggs, as many as four thousand."

"How can he do it?"

Away again, discussion and report of busy farms, of all
the arable lands and the people there singing in the
churches or preparing for the county fairs, the central
plains rolling off toward the Knobs and the eastern mountains. "Are people what they are because they live where
they do?"

"Huntsmen gather no strawberries out of the sea."

"Maybe the old order is the best. The fathers of the
country knew what they were about."

Logan at hand: "Let it be so. He'll make a pact with
his fellows. Hands around the sea. The Brush Grove
farmer has got to fight in his heart for the Serbian peasant
or the cattleman in Russia. God pity us!"

"What's the remedy, young man?" Drake asked. "What d'y'propose?"

A theory was stated, laid out boldly with long explanations. Thus and thus, different in detail from the theory of last week, but founded upon a man's oneness with his fellowmen, his fellowmen-ship. Deeper than his personal desire, there is in every man a need for his kind. Language itself depends upon a sharing of many men. No man ever made speech. The mind depends upon language, words, arranged images that have been named by other men, all men. . . . Man is a collective creature, a focus where many men, dead or living, come together. His tools came to him from many men, any tool you might name being built up of centuries of man-experience. . . . A world of shared experience would at last lead to a world of shared goods, shared comforts, shared security. Left to himself from birth a man would be a jittering animal. He spoke against Drake's mounting hostility, against his mounting anger, speaking louder, retelling his first argument which was best realized. Drake's lifted hand did not stop the flow of argument, his upward pointing index finger, his sunburned crumpled hand, his thin ruddy face, his flashing bleary eyes beneath his graying brows, his teeth biting at his hard cheek, his two hands gripping the arms of the chair.

"And what does your species Man look like?"

"Like any man, like you or me or Elkins. Any . . ."

"A general mug, an average jowl on the top of his neck. 'Good morning, Mr. Average,' he'll say. 'Pleased to meet y', Mr. Species.' It's all rot and nonsense."

An effort to modify, to restate. . . .

"Rot and drivel. He'd freeze to death in a winter and wait for food to crawl into his mouth. He's damned already, dead before ever he was borned. The lazy idiot wouldn't even have a name. Squat down and wait for It, your ALL, to put sop into his maw. Wants a job, he does. Job, JOB means a piece of work, a job-lot of work to tide him over the season. Moves on then to another job. Lives nowhere, owns nothing. Gets borned in a hospital provided by the ALL, buried the same way. Let 'im make himself a job. Clear out, I say. Get to work for yourself, Blunder-headed Species. Son-of-old-Adam. Fed up on pretties."

Quiet, and an attempt to restate some small part of the earlier matter, to withdraw the argument from overstatement and anger.

"You can't talk to me." A long blast on the horn brought a man from the stable. Three orders were given and a report stated. "Away with y'," and the man was gone, Drake then leaving the theory of man and the theorists, to stalk through his upper hall and over the bridge to his seat in the sun where he called orders to his barnyard.

Running in from the garden with her hands full of mint for Martha's julep, full of savory for her grandfather's relish, Jocelle kept a manifold mental state that was assembled of the bright weather of early summer, the forgotten and absented preacher, the secret manuscripts that lay above the secret *Cosmograph* in her lower drawer, of her pleasure in a new hair-dressing she had devised and in the summer cotton frocks she had sewed and fitted, of the sadness of Martha's lingering illness, of the touch of strong rough fingers on her throat to forbid her report of what was written and entrusted to her hiding, of the slow anapæst on the horn that called her. Thus fitted, she ran here and there, out to the mailbox to get the morning paper, out to the field where J.T. cut the clover to take the report. She could not stay long at the knitting.

Martha could knit endlessly, and the stockings grew behind her needles. Seeing her at the knitting, as she returned from the outside, Jocelle saw her aunt as if an emanation of clear-thinking stood about her when she spoke. Looking up suddenly from the needles and seeing her aunt thus, she cried out, half in laughter:

"What is it?"

"Logan."

"What's he, then?"

"He's a good animal."

A swift picture, a memory, constructed itself in the smooth tangles of knitted wool. She was looking down into a bramble, into a thicket of bushes and trees. Deep down a sloping space she once had seen a beautiful sleek polecat that looked sharply up at her, and while its gaze was fixed, it turned its head slowly in the dull shade of the bushes. The beast was still with terror of her. She could discover nothing out of this picture and from Martha's words, although she thought Martha always to be right.

The large black weasel, the animal of the thicket, was in some way like Logan. It had been for her a memorial of vanquished animal life brought back to the little jungle of the farm, frightened, trying to bring its two unfocused eyes to a unified vision.

She did not understand Martha then. Walking alone, having no counsel, she dressed herself in the flowered dress and bound her hair in the fashion used for girls. Thus guided she went unafraid into the presence of the avowed lover. He leaned above the old hound in the porch. His eyes seemed to be searching the ground for something, a habit derived from his occupation. Seeing the hardness of his mouth as it was drawn in denial or disdain, the roughness of his hands, the flinty, unyielding pursuit of his mind where it brought its protest to formulæ, she was vaguely joyous, knowing that she rested somewhere deeply within this troubled presence.

"A great deal will happen before it's done," he said, the war being in his mind. "They're momentarily sold out by prosperity. Expand, they will, beyond their bounds. They'll come to the end of it ruined by debt. It'll not last long, I said today at Mayfair Church. *Soils,* that was my topic, but I broke through. I let go and gave out what I had in mind. 'God, men,' I said, 'take care! How long do y' think this war'll last? Two years at the longest. After that, slump! Slump in farmstuff. Who'll pay then?' I said. 'How much do you owe since you bought ten more milch cows? How much since you bought fifty acres more to cultivate? God, men, let me tell you just once. Draw in. Take care.' "

He looked at her, seeing past her person, looking at some connection or some relation that lay between them, as of that day and of all time passed. He frowned, looking at her closely. "Jocelle, I might myself be a pent-up man. . . . When it's finished we'll then, maybe, will we? consider what it might be to finish out our lives together."

"Oh, yes."

"It'll be, what? Easy?"

"It'll be hard not to," she said.

Crying out her name, he bound her to himself with endearments, saying what he had said before, securing again her acquiescence. He continued speaking, a long, broken speech that returned to the first questioning. They walked away toward the highroad and stopped by the small thicket at the side of the pond. "I might be obliged to go far," he said. His outburst at Mayfair Church had been sudden. He could not determine what might come of it. Stopping to listen when she murmured some phrase, he continued. He had no taste to kill men, he said. His anger was misplaced, he supposed, and he laughed cruelly at his predicament. It, his anger, ought to find itself a personal enemy and thrust there and kill. There would be unpleasantness ahead, perhaps danger. His arms were withdrawn from her suddenly.

There was more than one thing to consider, he continued, speaking slowly. There were three things, as he looked at it, and he drew his hat low over his eyes as if he would consider these things alone, his gaze fixed on the distant hills behind the house. Declaring that he would go, he still lingered, saying: "We'll not touch on it further."

She acquiesced to all that he offered and denied. Words were sufficient guaranty, split into infinite degrees, with content inherent in each fine transition from particle to particle. Affection and pleasure were put back into the word, any word, by which a plan might be suggested or a confidence confirmed.

He was gone without further approach to the near matter. He had left her a manuscript, saying that it was a substitute for the first he had left her, that it further developed his first contention. Reading the document through to the end, she found that he had written there a phrase, "Committed to the care of my beloved," and she was pleased that he was not afraid of grandeur and that he approached their love with conscious dignity. She closed the papers and held them closely in her hands in a passion of acquiescence, wanting him to have whatever it was that he desired—his perfect democracy never yet seen upon the earth, communal being in which all shared, yielding him this and all in a passion of consent. The word became the fleshly substitute and memory the guaranty. While he was gone, the days passed in expectation. At hand again, and his reticence suggested all that had been spoken in the portico or beside the pond, or written beyond the social theory. His dainty admiration rested in confidence upon her.

Words were compressed. Without themselves there was much excitement among the farms. Between them discussion now was passed by, the gentle admiring glance and the unspoken understanding being the substitute, movement receding minute point by minute point through the intensities of unstated meanings, the withheld gesture. They were waiting for something to be resolved, as if they waited for some external cataclysm to break, resting now upon a plane of general liking and affectionate admiration —the gift of a book or a package of flower seeds, the secret reticences of greeting or departure, the light touch of a hand on her fingers.

VI

WALTER came back for a three days' visit before he sailed with the marines. Early in the morning he was riding the old stallion up and down the track. There was incessant talk, and the labor of the farm dragged. No blasts were blown on the horn. The men sitting on the bridge offered endless reasonings:

The need for a Concourse of Nations. No nation shall dominate the whole mass. None dominate the seas. Intelligent international intercourse. Fair dealings. Fight for peace without victory.

Query: Where do you think you're going?

"God knows, and he hasn't told me. I'll sail with the marines."

"War. What is the war?"

Called down to the diningroom, there would be but scant interruption.

"What you say. Give Walter a glass of my white grape, Jocelle. Out of the little black cask. Give a seat here beside me. Tell Nettie Tobin to bring in the dinner."

The meat carved in sweet decorum, anxieties as to what meat is preferred, what sauce, what bread. Gathered together, four about the board, Dickon being gone, Martha keeping her bed. "Let Jocelle sit beside me," the soldier called out. His face was large and drawn, hearty and distraught. His eyes were strange when they were not laughing. He laughed in loud bursts of guffaw, and leaned later to his plate to eat in gusts of hunger. "Let Jocelle sit here beside me."

J.T. moved away, and Jocelle came around the board to sit near him. He drew his arm through her arm and drank his wine thus. "I want a woman beside me until I pitch off at the dock. . . ."

"When you come back . . ."

"It's unlikely I'll ever come back. It's just now begun and I'll be there early. Where's Jocelle gone? I want a woman with me until I pitch off the pier."

"Green beans with jowl meat, broiled chicken, have some, young man."

"General Smuts in East Africa. Nobody knows what's on in Russia. Vimy Ridge. Advances between the Somme and . . . Ypres . . . Wypers is good enough for me. All is, I know I'm on my way."

"Young man, your great-grandfather was at the Battle of Tippecanoe."

"I'm damned if I knew the old boy."

"Your great-great-grandfather was in Boone's Fort. Held the country against the aborigines."

"Sing, sing, somebody sing."

"He was . . ."

"Sing 'Love Me and the World Is Mine.'"

"I know where I'm going. I know what's there. I've found out. Western Front, it's all one, north or some other. Machine-guns in concrete pill-boxes. A front line out ahead, your enemy, safe in concrete, rigged up to send hell across at a rate of, say, five hundred balls a minute. Don't I know? Liquid fire. Quick as hell. You're tired of it all. You want to burst your head open against a stone. You can't surrender to a machine-gun. Walk up and say: 'S'nough, old pal! Kamerad!' Machine. Here's my hand up. Crawl in a shell-hole and die with the hungry rats if you're not already dead twice over with your guts one place and your brains another. If my bullet would only come! you think. Here it comes now, oh, God! Your own buddie on the ground, his legs shot off. Tries to crawl off. . . . Face gone, maybe. It's fun to scrub the kitchen. Teach sense to a lot of white trash. Deloused, disloused, that is to say. Bailey is my buddie, and Tremont. Not a man in the whole company under five foot ten. Say, you'll see a bunch of go-getters when you see Company blank, my unit. Duty first and then pleasure. Target practices. There's not a blame blasted son-of-a-bitch in the whole

157

company can crack 'em off neater than yours truly, Walter Drake, esquire, candidate for corporal, hooray! Pass me the chicken again. It's war, though, you understand."

They went out to the cattle pens to see the calves. Twenty fine baby beeves to fatten in the autumn, standing now at the gate waiting to be let into the small pasture, where they would nibble daintily at the tender early-summer herbs, preferring milk, being scornful as yet of the grass. The herd had been four times multiplied to meet the demands of the war.

"The old man did a good job."

"Substituted beef stock for the fine bloods."

"Old man got good sense after all. . . ."

"Founder the whole lot on white clover, if you don't watch."

"Watch is what the old man does, though."

Up in the far pasture walking, the heat of the day spread about as if it were a solid in which the fresh green plants stood fixed and still. The young leaves glistened in the sun that took dampness slowly out of them, but they yielded without stint. There were hours of merciless heat, in which the leaves had not yet hardened. In the still twilight the frogs in the pond cried incessantly. Walter was restless at the front gallery, wanting to walk away into the

dusk, calling Jocelle. She would go with him out toward
the pond, her white dress becoming vague and dim as she
went from the portico into the faintly powdered dark.
Martha above stairs leaned in the deep window ledge to
look out upon the fireflies in the grass. Old Drake in the
portico, sitting with J.T., and the hour passed toward the
deepening of the dark in the sky and the coming of the
stars. He flung out a blast on his horn, two short and a
long note, and Jocelle gathered into the vague dark at the
side of the pond and came forward, a pale white shadow
that laughed with Walter, coming back quickly over the
gravel way.

Martha was above at the window. Her seeing enhanced
by the dark of the room behind her, she could see the light
and the dark figures as they walk out of the gray-black
of the night, as they came brilliantly into the segment of
light from the lower hall. Their chairs scraped on the floor
of the porch and they were seated. Vague laughter. Logan
came down the driveway in his old car. Loud voices, the
sounds distended to build up some remote reality. Before
leaving, Logan went up the stairs to greet her, Jocelle
bringing a small light. Walter wandered through the
house, never wanting to go to his bed in the west room
below stairs, never wanting to be left alone on the porch.
He was lonely, desolate, dreading departure, wanting to
be already gone. Up before the dawn, he would be tossing
down hay with J.T. and Elkins.

"God! I never thought I'd live to see the day I'd be sorry to leave this place.

"God, I'm still here. I dreamed I was gone just now.

"What's the French for bridge?

"*Pons,* I reckon, *Le pons* . . .

"I'll never take time to learn how the Frogs talk. I'll be busy. Hell, I'll be busy!

"Back to breakfast. Forward march. Squad right . . . hep, hep, bacon and eggs!" They march twenty steps over the green toward the house and fall out of step. They pass in at the western doorway.

Jocelle came in at the door from the hall. She began to work with the pitchers and to pour water into the glasses. "How can I ever get at the thing unless I land in France? I want the thing here in my hands here, now. I'd break it in two with my fist. God! I want to get at grips with the thing. My feet are here, still. Firm land." He passed the first serving to Jocelle. "Here, Nettie, get Jocelle the silver cup off the sideboard. Pour her out the first. I want a woman with me until I kick off at the dock and ring a farewell bell to America."

It was the day of his departure. The last breakfast. There was no repose. They were on their feet and back in their chairs again. "Thought is a fool. A man ought to have the top part of his head cut off, razed, what d'y'call it? Circumcised? Excised is the word. Cut off." He ate greedily all that was brought before him and sat back, careless of his napkin. Drake poured him a cup of the white wine.

"Can't Martha come down? I want my family here to hear me talk. Call Martha."

They would be in the parlor before the south windows. "Play 'Casey Jones,'" he called to Jocelle, but he did not wait to hear the tune played through. "Play 'Love Me and the World Is Mine.'"

Calling Martha up the stairs, and her weak voice answered him from her doorway. He would linger a moment at her door while she lay resting in the bed.

"The submarines pitching hell into the bottom of steel-crusted ships. What's save-Belgium? Jocelle, where's she at? I want my woman with me, at my side, till I pitch head first down the everlasting gangway."

On the stairs, going down to meet Jocelle at the bottom. Martha's voice calling in terror over the tread of his feet: *"Morituri te salutant."*

The cry was low and slow-spoken, forgotten soon after in the confusion of speeches in the lower hall, in the portico. He was drunk with distress and farewells. "Go over the farm the last time." They were out on the green before the door, their voices floating farther away as they dispersed, Drake within to the upper bridge to call Elkins with the horn. Uneven footsteps went away toward the back of the house and farther. "Call Jocelle, I want a woman with me while I wait," and the bleat of the horn. two short blasts and a long, the —— —— —————— sounded from the bridge above. Jocelle came from the kitchen door and walked away with him, going toward the rear of the farm.

Morituri te salutant, blown faintly from the hot summer afternoon, remembered as spoken down the stairs, and Jocelle walked out across the withering heat and over the haunted grass that had not yet wilted, it being still full of new spring life. "This war, it'll slip into another without a break. You'll see. What're we here for? The young, born now, they'll ask it. God, I'm still here. I thought I was gone. I thought I went yesterday." He was continually talking. They went outward across the pasture toward the cool shadows near the creek.

———

Jocelle came in from the wild summer afternoon. None met her on the stairs. She was faintly delirious, and being hurt she mounted the steps with difficulty. Her limbs trembled with exhaustion and she lay in her room, across the way from the room Martha used, having locked her door. Drake walked through the hall to the front portico, where he stood to cry farewells to Walter as the car that had come to convey him away throbbed on the driveway not far from the door. Jocelle did not go from her bed. None called to her.

There were cries outside. Elkins was called from the stable. Martha called from the upper window.

"We won't forget y'."

"You'd better, and quick as y'can."

"God bless y'," Drake called.

"Bring my belt . . . My sack . . . Where's Elkins? . . . Bring it . . . Good-by, Elkins. See you in Purgatory. ⁄ . .

"Good-by, Wade. Good-by, Uncle. See you too in hell."

"God bless y'. God keep y'."

"Good-by, Elkins. Meet me in hell. Good-by, Tobin . . . see you later. See you later."

When he was gone, the house was very still. Each one seemed to have gone to his accustomed place to brood and rest. Jocelle, falling to sleep at last, contrived a picture of ease, in which the war had left her and had gone to some farther battlefield. Lying still afterward, when her brief sleep had passed, contemplating now the despairing act of the departing soldier, it seemed to her, brooding on the nature of man, that the war had rolled its waves forward to include herself, to float her back into itself on the tides of her own spent and angry flesh. Herself seemed divided into three. The person of yesterday, the girl careful of her ailing aunt and heedful of her grandfather's call, the slim laughing creature of the house and the fields;

this one was crushed under the load of physical apathy and pain, of humility and confusion of ends. Another arose from moment to moment, stepping through the confusion in strong rhythmic stride, asserting itself, unafraid and unashamed, saying nothing but biding her time. This one made one quick decision, final and deeply seated, as if it flowed with her own rhythmic presence, less than a whisper, known to her members and her flesh: she would not see Walter again until she had known her own lover; she would have her own; she would be vindicated. She would hate Walter more entirely as the days passed, contriving deeper hatred, and John Logan would join her in hate. There was argument and confusion and semi-delirium.

The third person answered fitfully but with ordered thinking when she was allowed a voice in the general confusion, saying: "It will be right. There will be the new earth, like the old in outline. . . . Grandfather will sound the horn, the two short bleats and the one long. . . . I will go up to the cabin with an order . . . 'Tell Tobin . . . Get the book with the brown cover . . . Get the notes out for Perkins . . . Ask . . . Take . . .' I will be watching the papers for reports of the war, I, Jocelle, whole again. In town, the girls, my friends, some of them married. Rose with two children. Celia gone to work in Louisville. The old world, as formerly, myself in it. It would be some other, the lover, she contrived, not this dishonored and frightened incestuous ruffian that tore away the curtains of friendship and fraternal affection. The other voices speaking, panic followed, and she lay for many hours, through the day and the night.

She gathered the torn and soiled clothing from her wardrobe and rolled them into a tight bundle. She wanted to dispose of them finally, so that she need never see them again. She wanted to put them by completely and without further delay, in this act to bring to an end, insofar as she could, all visible reminders of the act of violence. The clothing bound into a bundle, she went secretly out through the farm to the wooded tangles along the creek. Here she made a small fire of the paper wrappings and some dry sticks and slowly burned the cloth, a small part at a time. The burning left a stain on the ground in the woods, and this she covered with a few stones, carried from the creek, but, the fire covered, the stones were still present as a mark or a sign. In an agony of despair she carried the stones back to the creek bed and left the dark scar of the burning clearly visible, trusting that the rains would obliterate much of it and the late summer vegetation would spring up to hide the rest.

Drake would sit in the diningroom or, taking thought of the needs of the fields, he would walk briskly into the hall and up the stairway. He would sometimes stop at

Martha's room to ask after her health. "And what did the doctor say to that? The man of medicine, what does he now hold?" Then he would go down the long hall to the opened door, across the bridge, and out into the bright sunlight. The sharp blast on the horn or the cry of the bell told of him at the lookout place. The clatter of feet was remembered after he was gone. He being themselves in essential acts and opinions, he being the outspoken act, calling defiance for all from the upper bridge. After the bleat of his horn, feet would come swiftly from the barns. Summer outside, and the corn two feet high would be arising beyond the need of the plow. The birds in the tall oak trees about the house were high placed, and their cries were far away, spreading above the house among the upper limbs and branches. Wrens were nesting within the crevice of a partly closed shutter, swallows thundering into the east chimney at dusk or out again at dawn.

Lying in the semi-dark of the shuttered room, the west room above stairs, Jocelle would be thinking in feverish jargon of the summer, the world outside the farm where war was being prepared. Encampments, enlistments, embarkments, military jargon, war readiness, propaganda to enlist citizen action. In the barnyard behind the stable a hen was cackling, having laid an egg, screaming over the monstrous awfulness of the thing she had done; she had continued life. Through these ready reports and present confusions went a constant theme that ran on a

continuous thread—herself, her life, from the first remembered mists of knowing to the present. It swung outward
in a curve and arrived at the present moment, making a
sharp thrust, including all of time as known to her. She
leaped from the bed and snatched a few garments from
her closet, thrusting them upon her indignant body. Out
in the pasture she walked far in the sun of mid-day. Among
some far trees, in a little thicket grown lightly with thorn
bushes, she sat in the rank grass. Farther, on a plowed
hill, she walked to the place where one lone tree, blasted
by lightning, stood partly stripped of branches, the nesting place of ravens or turkey-hawks.

With the passing of the days she entered a delirium in
which she thought that she would give birth to some
further monstrosity of war, as if war would tear a Gargan-
tuan, incestuous birth through her breast. War, clothed
in flesh but horrible with cries of peace, with abstract
ameliorations, endless successions of war doubled upon
war to make a child in the likeness of the father; violent
and fearful, self-justifying, religious in preparation for
battle, it forgave itself even while it worked tremendous
ruin upon the earth.

She arose and dressed herself and went to the farther of
the two tenant cabins, the house beyond the creek, where
she found the mulatto woman named Geril, wife of one
of the laborers. Sitting in quiet she heard the woman
talk. War lay here as a delicate iambic rhythm told in sim-

ple words, unknown in its blood and clamor. Sitting
within the shadows of the house the woman talked neg-
ligently of the life she had led while she mended an old
garment. Half amused at what she said, half fearful, as if
she were conscious of being lascivious, the woman told
of nursing the sick, of caring for the new-born, of going
places in secret to midwife secret birth. That which the
woman deemed fearful or evil was thrown swiftly from her
lips and followed by a scraping laughter. The woman's
starched skirts crinkled when she sat into her low chair.
Jocelle went there again and again, day after day. Seven
ill-tended children ran about the door or cared for the
least one of themselves as it lay on an old quilt on the grass.
This Geril told obscene stories of the town, of the neigh-
borhood, stories which Jocelle would not entirely believe,
but she accepted the medium in which they moved, making it actual as an unfearful fact that touched herself. Thus
she learned, distilled from the tales of this one, that there
need be no further physical distress beyond that which she
had already borne. She was unappeased in her anger and
hate, but unafraid.

When Logan came to the farm, she slipped quietly back
into some remote place, a tangle of bushes along the creek,
or the farther hill of the blasted tree. She had no further
need of Geril and so she went no more to the cabin, un-

less she went there on some mission relating to the fowl.
She would come softly back from her retreat at the fall
of night, listening for voices, and she went slowly about
her accustomed tasks. She had gone now outside the prevailing reality as she had experienced it formerly, as she
knew it. Any care for the adornment of her person seemed
far from her, and if she brushed her hair or tended her
skin, these offices were performed without heart. Voices
seemed flat and meaningless as Mrs. Tobin spoke of the
roasting of a fowl or the baking of a cake. Senseless con-
cerns surrounded her. The preparations for war cluttered
the newspapers with futile words which she read without
attention and forgot. If she tried to bring herself to an
interest in the things of girls—a bright new cotton dress or
a ribbon—in adornments to attract the admiration of her
lover, her thought slipped from these in apathetic loathing
and she was left staring at her face in the mirror, at the
mechanism and not the charm of eyes, or the violet shading of the iris, at the dreary evidences of life beneath the
eye and about the moving muscles of the mouth.

Up into the east chamber, where Martha lay on the bed
or sat in a corner of a sofa by the window, Jocelle went
with a soft egg and a pitcher of milk. The supper below
was over. The sunset poured under the trees and over the
outside wall in a steady stream. Martha kept a continual

brightness in her eyes, a fierce eagerness in her gaze when it was lifted from her books.

"What is it?" Jocelle asked from the doorway.

"The milk is good," she said, smiling her gratitude for the care Jocelle gave.

"What else is good?"

"There's a mort of good and evil. Take your hand off the door handle. A hand on a door signifies going. You're gone so much lately. Don't go. Why didn't you tell me Johnnie Briggs shaved away his hair to please you?"

"It didn't please me."

"Samson. I saw how he cut the tree into splinters. Shorn locks no matter."

Jocelle smiled to assist the sport, not caring.

"The barefoot friar, the scullery priest, can fall into a desire for the virgin of the house, will dare lift his eyes to the king's daughter and lay himself out in a speech of gallantry. What a piece man is! He shaved it off to please the one virgin of the house."

"It was the war," Jocelle said, "confused Briggs, maybe."

She stood beside the door, her hand away from the latch. She had been all day among the fields beating about in the light late-summer winds. She had inspected the orchard trees to see if they were ready for the third spraying. She had carried a message to the tenant house where Geril was setting hens for brooding the late supply of kitchen fowl. Returning, she had bent her path from the way, wanting

170

not to see the blackened stain in the woods near the creek,
wanting to see that the stain had been obliterated. Wanting to see that she might not see, she had walked a half-
mile through the creekside tangles.

"The milk is good," Martha said. "And you are red from
the winds. Two winds, I said. You are gathering the roses
while you may."

The turmoil that had been partly allayed returned. "Do
you want anything more?" Jocelle asked, wanting to be
gone.

"A letter from Walter," Martha said, opening a ragged
envelope to take out a flimsy sheet.

"I didn't know there was a letter," Jocelle said. She had
been gone when the mail was brought. Wanting to see if
the scar in the woods was gone, she had walked fearfully
out of any path, to come upon the place by accident. Coming thus upon the letter, she waited to hear. The scar in the
grass under the trees had not been obliterated. Martha was
reading. He had landed somewhere safely. A drum-beat of
drill, drill, drill, sounded in the reading voice, work, target
practice . . . Wanting not to hear it, she wanted still to
have done with the hearing. She closed her eyes and stayed
her hand against the frame of the door.

" 'Show me the damned what-is-it and I'll shoot fifty holes
straight into the blistered bed-buggy scab. . . . Lice already. Little bitches that bite your brisket. Run then to
hide in the seams of your drawers. . . . Come to' (word

erased) 'and went by' (erasures). 'Food very good, but all tastes like beans, mostly beans. . . . Had a girl in' (erasure) 'but let her go when I came on. . . . Should worry . . . get me another in' (erasures). . . . 'Took three in' (erasure) 'where a Frenchman said to me "Parley Voo." "Peace Parley," I said back. "Show me the war, you blasted Frog," I said. "Show me the damned what-for and I'll shoot seventeen giddy bullets into the hind parts of the thing." Marie was her name in' (erasure) 'but she called herself Fleurette in' (erasure) 'and was a lousy widow with two husbands already in No-Man's Land. When I come back I'll mend all the damage ever I did and marry all the war widows, God help me do it.'

"You are strange in the eyes," Martha said.

How to tell Martha. She did not know. Asking herself what words one would employ to tell an aunt that her mind had been seared by the rending of her body in a loveless embrace put upon her by a frantic, careless, frightened, fouled, war-shocked man, in fervor of impatience and imaginings. It seemed imperative to speak now, to begin some telling which might bring word of her distress to Logan, who, it seemed now, after the passing of the summer weeks, had been unconcerned for her hiding, content to send messages, notes, manuscript theories of government, redress of wrong, warning to the farmer, written into cramped pages and left for her on Martha's table. Wanting to bring an end to these dull and negative interchanges, her mind being empty of every wish to please, wanting to set nothing beside nothing and make an end, she began to speak.

She sat near the door on a stiff chair, leaning forward, her arms hanging beyond her knees. Crying out, then: "Fleurette, she called herself . . . Marie . . . Anybody . . . Jocelle . . . Wiped his dirty filth on my body. The day he went away."

Martha turned slightly and looked out the window. She looked, her head slightly lowered, her gaze fixed on the ground under the trees below. Her gaze seemed to travel along the ridge of her thin nose to strike at length the base of a tree where the shaded grass grew thin. She and her look were one, herself now become a focused line from eye to tree. She spoke at last, slowly.

"You are, then, what they call a war bride, a holy woman. . . . Bride of the state."

"I didn't want to be. I won't be. I wanted to be myself."

"A holy woman," Martha said. She spoke quietly. The quiet of the house followed the quiet of her words, and a long delay divided her first utterance from what followed. She lay on the bed, pale and wasted, her brown hair more gray as the year advanced. Her thin hands were drawn together to lie folded above her dressing gown. She spoke of the common social mind, the ultimate good, the national defense, the one fervor that all shared.

173

"The fury of the war broke upon you. Battlegrounds brought withindoors . . ." She was still speaking. "You didn't stop to think what that meant. Woman espoused of the Nation."

The evening began to fall into twilight. The grackles had ceased to chime in the tall trees outside. "Let the days pass," Martha said. Kindness would come out of the passing of time. Emptiness had already settled about these words ahead of their speaking. Jocelle, empty of content, of hurt, of purpose, heard the heavy utterance. The words fell slowly from spent lips. The war was spread into every cove and hollow, over every hill. Fields and gardens and hamlets knew it, garret and diningroom and cellar. The war, known thus, far and wide, spread far from Jocelle, and she walked slowly about in the twilight, standing by the window, stopping by the mantel. Divided from the wide flow of the war, she was emptied of feeling, and a numbness to all relations and affections, to all present hurts and physical distresses, had long settled over her. The crown of her head seemed to float in the air, a foot above her eyes. "It is a curious thing, the infantile ego," Martha said. "As if anyone were better or more sacred than another until proved so by some deed." She seemed amused at the world. Its minor hurts and blessings were scarcely worth the weary lifting of a hand from repose on the front of a blue wool gown, pale blue, faded to smoke by many cleansings. She opened her eyes and spoke suddenly, flash-

ing truth at Jocelle as one flung a kite up into the wind.
"It won't seem green, the wound, after a little. There's the
other consideration." She flung the last out joyously and
flashed a smile that followed the words, and a sudden up-
lifted sweep of her thin fingers.

"There's something else."

"What?"

"Bride of the War-Madness! . . . You've got, you,
everything. What more do you want?"

"I didn't want to be . . ."

"You might as well be such as any other. . . . What
did you want then? Sacred to old man Drake's toom-to-
tooooom horn. Married to a fox-call. Go on away. Play
pretty Poll and clatter-clatter laughter, prunes and prisms.
Let the roof fall in on y'. Whine and drivel over your tissue-
paper wreckage. Old man Drake himself, yourself."

"What did I ever do to harm you?"

"He drove away my lover. 'Whore, strumpet,' he called
me. I didn't forget, not for one day." She cried out, beating her fingers together.

Jocelle was quiet, standing beside the window. She did
not know now on what plane she might rest nor where
justice stood. She was alone, as she had entered the room,
as she had been alone when she sat beside the door to tell
her story. The night darkened and she brought Martha's
lamp. They seemed to be moving on unrelated parallels,
scarcely communicating. Jocelle brought a pitcher of

water, and Martha got up from the bed to sit in the chair at her bedside, wrapping her blanket about her feet.

"You might tell Logan," she said. "His big blubbering heart is well-nigh broken over the war-madness anyway."

"I'll tell my own in my own time," Jocelle answered.

Martha had taken back her tears, had swallowed them in her thin throat. She seemed light, flinging up her hand, crying out, half screaming, as a bird in the air making a last flight. "The war is a witch," she said. "War Witch, I thank thee. Thou hast taught me a good phrase. Takes maidens for her lemans. Lesbian, they call her. Makes witches out of her maids. . . . Run along. Eat your cake and have it. Tell Mrs. Tobin to set some yeast for light rolls tomorrow. Run along. You don't need me. Wedlock and flintlock and shotgun marriages. Run on."

In the diningroom Jocelle wrote letters for her grandfather or she worked at the invoices. Drake searched his papers, his eyes lowered, and he spoke in an even tone, scarcely audible: sixteen head young shoats; nine calves, Jersey, young heifers; eleven bull calves; five mule colts. "Write June fifth for the sale date for three mules. . . ." Thus and forward. She scarcely lifted her eyes to watch him as he spoke the numbers, as he numbered his flocks and herds for the war tax. He was not of the earth which he numbered. Through the even recital which was dictated, through the quiet house, the afternoon quiet of the farm, the indifferent going of Elkins about the mid-afternoon chores of the stables, of Mrs. Tobin setting the kitchen in order, of the monotonous crying of the crickets that were hidden about the fireplace, through her own insensate attention which wrote the items correctly but gave them no meanings, there went one active, evil, brutal knowledge that took shape in the indifferent medium through which it rode. It was impassioned, shaped now into a sign, the War-Witch. It went on some widely spread and permeating spiritual being. It was evil. It was beyond knowing.

Days passed, flowing without monotony, for the people of the farm made a difference between one day and another. She wrote the items of sale and entered each new-born animal. Men came to Drake to borrow money. Everything that could be spared was sent away from the farm to help feed the armies or the people of the towns. Elkins was seen sweeping out an old unused cornroom to make it ready to hold grain.

She tried to assume the real of things, to place herself again in the life illusion. She took from her drawer a length of bright cloth to whip herself into an interest in its value. Holding the cloth before her body, she draped it in folds and drew it together about her form, planning a dress of it. The rose flowers printed on the field of brown brought a faint flush to her cheeks and a deeper red to her mouth. Indifferent, she saw these appearances come to her face, telling herself that, if she would but cut out the frock, interest in wearing it might follow. Later she fell to studying the thread of the weave, seeing past the color and illusion of flowers, and seeing the in and out of the threads as they lapped together, the futile makeshift of man as he took the down of plants and tried thus to conceive a covering for his shrinking body and his trembling spirit. The cloth lay on the floor of her room for a day and was later thrust back into a drawer.

Logan came from the upper counties, and thus he would be frequently at the farm. Word of his being at hand would come to Jocelle with a summons from Martha, and she would leave whatever task she had assumed to go to the room where Martha lay. Logan seemed large here as not perfectly remembered, but his tread was light on the carpet and his voice subdued, his large frame filling Martha's chair. Illusion was gone from him and thus he sat, plain to see, graceful in the moving of limbs. His hair was wavy with the damp days of early autumn. Sitting in the light of Martha's window, listening to her slow story, his eyes were mossy brown with green tones in the pigment. His eyes were quick and bright and seemed contrary to his slow-spoken speech as if his words were belated comment on opinions that were already stated. If he looked beyond the window, a distress gathered about his eyes. He was positive in manner, as formerly, but he sometimes contradicted his earlier statement. Inaction gnawed at half-cruel lines about his lips, a continual dissent and rebellion. He was not of the kind, she saw, to fling himself, altogether, against whatever thwarted him; he would yield himself in small fragments, lasting out the end. Returning from his excursions into prophecy and dissent, he would be taking forward some story of his last journey. Miles of travel over lumpy roads, speeches, conversations, war thrift, war magic, politics, the men in the camps—these mingled with the banter he carried for Martha's sake. If Jocelle offered to leave, he would be at the door before her.

"Make her stay," he would call to Martha, catching at the shrinking shoulders and flying hands. He would be asking her to stay, in one way or another. And Martha:

"Stay, Jocelle. But she's sure to be wanted. The barn or the kitchen or the letter box or the bridge. She's the good fairy of the farm."

As the good fairy of the farm, the war bride, the War Witch, Jocelle sat on a stool near the fireplace.

Logan's apprehension for the farmers had grown into theories of peace. He had felt a mob hostility to his opinions where they did not fall within the prevailing sentiment. He touched but a little on these matters. When Martha held up a colored print showing the flag of the country stiffly spread, he saluted it with his right hand.

"Right or wrong, still my country."

There was smiling and sad laughter. He spoke quietly,

without anger. The young of every second or third generation would be sacrificed, he said, the boys and girls, for the girls would not escape if the boys were to go. He talked of peace, of built-up malice, built-up revenge. "Let a few be killed and you'll see." Fear and vindication, then revenge. War readiness . . .

Jocelle sat shrinking, fearful that some caprice of the sick woman might fling out her titles with harsh explanations. He would be telling of his friend, Joel Hagan. Had she read Hagan's defiant speech? It was among the papers he had sent her in September. She had not read it and she looked toward the near blaze and glow of the fire. Hagan had refused to do combatant service, had refused to take military instructions. He had addressed the men in camp, gathering them about him in small groups. He himself, Hagan, gone to camp, had cried out warning to the poor again and again. Hagan had been sent now to Fort Leavenworth to be segregated. Nothing more came from him now.

Looking at him then while he talked with Martha, Jocelle saw his bent head that was turned sidelong from her, telling of Joel's plight, his degraded reputation among his fellows, his despised name. She shrank toward the hearth and joined mentally the pure blaze that arose from the burning coals, turning her shoulder from the disaster at Leavenworth, the threat to Logan, the inevitable violence. Looking at him while he talked with Martha, but

180

clinging mentally to the certainty of the fire beside which she sat on a low stool which placed her much lower than his face, she saw him in an unfamiliar plane. His teeth seemed long as he spoke. His lips curled in sadness and distress that became a snarl. She could scarcely attend to what he said, so great was her concentration upon his appearance in saying it. He looked toward her once with a smile, speaking meanwhile, fixing his gaze upon her, waiting for her response. She gave it at length to liberate herself from his look.

Back at these opinions, and he seemed to thrust about, his muscles jerking with eagerness. Actually he was almost still. His hands lay on the arms of the chair. Martha shared his strangeness now, and it seemed to Jocelle that they devised something between them. Seen from below, his lower teeth were long, his body spread obliquely. She was about to cry out in terror and anger. She pressed her hands against the floor and partly arose.

He struck the chair suddenly with his fist, making some argument. His hands made the motions of waves rolling, three passes along the air, and some symbol of waves was stressed to make a point of what he was saying. He was lost in distress, steeped in despair. "I may have to leave this place," he said, half whispering.

"The conscientious objector," Martha said.

"No."

"The Insincere Objector . . ."

"What a word to describe a man!"

His face was frightful with pain, drawn downward, his mouth distorted. A damp sweat made a bright sheen on his brow when he turned suddenly toward the light. He made some hurried reply to Martha and went toward the door, bending slightly forward. He passed Jocelle without seeing her where she stood half arising from the stool by the fire. She stood at the door and saw him passing swiftly down the stairs. He did not look back when she called Martha in her distress. Below he went to his car and, when he had backed noisily around in the paddock, he went quickly away.

Thus until a night in winter when the frost had settled over the Kentucky rolling plains. Jocelle had carried a metal ewer of water above for Martha's bath. As she walked back and forth from the diningroom to the pantry, clearing the supper table, the door flapped in sibilance after her passing as if it were the wing of a bat. Drake kept his seat at the table and, when the dishes were cleared away, he kept his wine glass among the papers that were soon flung over the board.

Drinking his wine slowly, while J.T. and Dickon had gone outside or above, while the noises of the house throbbed faintly in the kitchen or in the rooms overhead, he looked toward Jocelle, watching her swift movements. She was preparing the room for the brief after-supper interval. "Jocelle!" he cried out suddenly, calling her back from the pantry door. "Jocelle, what is this war?"

"Where is it? Why today it's, as far as I know, mostly around the Adriatic. The Italians and the Austrians."

"What's it for? What'll it come to? What is it?"

"I can't tell. Me? How do I know? A higher price for eggs today. Poultry high. Everything high. Thirty cents a yard for a mean little piece of coarse cotton cloth to make Martha a slip."

"Thirty cents for a mean little yard of coarse cloth. What else?"

"Millions of people together to act in unison. That's something you wouldn't see without a war. I don't know what else. Some few outside the act. Ruin for the farmers, some say. They'll lose their land. One says it's so. Says win or lose we're ruined. . . . J.T. says, 'Right or wrong, still my country.' "

A sudden burst of hate sent a burning flush to her face. Hate stiffened all the flesh about her mouth. "Violence," she said. "Men mad at life because they're about to leave it. A man you hate drags you to a flat ledge and piles stones on you. Chokes your cry back in your throat. Struggle until your breath gives out. 'I'm on my way to battle,' he says. Your fingernails torn out by the roots. That's what it

183

means. My tongue pulled out of my throat and thrown out to the hound dogs behind the kitchen. A man with tusks that stick out of his jaw. On his way to battle, stopped to say good-by."

"Walter, I reckon," he said.

"On his way to battle. Wiped off his filth on me. That's what war means."

He drank slowly of the wine, staring at the corner of the room, his nether lip pursed upward at the middle and downward at the corners. She thought he was about to laugh, but his eyes at the moment became sad, the lids drooping. She was trembling in hatred and distress that she had spoken, and she moved farther toward the shadowed corner of the room.

Dickon came slowly down the stairs from the back upper room, and he sat slowly in a chair beside the hearth. He began to mend the fire and his broad angular shoulders were shivering as he tended the blaze. "What is this and all that to a man indoors forever?" she was asking within.

Dickon began to speak while he still busied himself with the fire-irons: "The Old Man of the Sea." He spat a long thread of tobacco into the ashes. "Crawls up on dry land. War then. Sacred Americans, sacred Britons, sacred Dutchmen, all in sacred battle. Roars like forty thousand devils let loose."

J.T. had come from the outside. He rattled papers under the lamp, reading again the press news from the war fronts.

"A patch of dragon's teeth," Dickon said, muttering. "Flung a handful into the ocean. Old Man of the Sea. Crawled up on land . . ."

Jocelle looked at J.T., at his bent head, at his eyes lowered to the print, his gaze drooping out of protruding eyeballs, himself bent in a half-circle about the table. Cupped thus to drink in the war, she saw as he saw, and seeing thus, the war was brought to general statements of objective and sector, activity and quiet. The men were not thus any part of it. They were a folly that accompanied it wherever it went. They attended to another, to the business of death and dying. A swift burst of clear-seeing accompanied her gaze upon J.T's. fixed, drooping stare. She saw a house in a wreck and burning. Before the house were ditches that had been yielded to the enemy's fire. It was their house, any house. The air overhead was full of screaming. There was water in ditches, running or still. Man had crept back into the seams of the earth, wanting to be a rat, to be a snake, to be a mole. He died there of his own filth, and the rats ate the last of him. Overhead the air was on fire with the hell he had made. Dickon was asking:

"Who was the wife of Mars, now? I disremember. She got ready his chariot for battle, greased the wheels. Drove his horses, some said. Came into battle with flyen hair. A torch or a firebrand in her fist. In one hand a whip. Drove on the combat. Jeered on the fighters. Bellona, I recall now was her name. Bellona. Some said his wife and some

185

said his sister, or his daughter. Incest for you again, and that's Greek too. Sister, mother, daughter, it's all one, no matter. His woman. Bellona."

Jocelle looked thus at the monster and at the woman near him.

"The war bride. War widows they say now. Bellona." Dickon called out again.

"What's become of Johnnie Briggs?" J.T. asked, as if he would change the trend of speaking. "He hasn't been seen, hair nor hide, since April."

"Nettie Tobin said Jocelle would know what went with 'im.''

Drake was still now, inattentive of what the others were saying. He seemed flushed and tremulous, and he gazed at first one object and then another, changing his position suddenly.

"Maybe Johnnie Briggs went away to the army. Did you, Jocelle, send Johnnie Briggs away to war?" J.T. asked, lightly teasing.

"Bellona," Dickon cried out. "Bellona. Sent a man away to battle. Jocelle sent a man out—warrior to fight for the country. Gave her blessen. Came here with his whiskers cleaned offen his face and some said made offers to Jocelle. She sends 'im away then to do battle for the land."

J.T. was laughing. He turned to his paper, but he looked up suddenly to laugh again.

"Gave a soldier's blessen and sent away to fight. Mars.

186

That's the idea. Johnnie Briggs is Mars, say. Strong man, too. I saw when he cut a tree down with the ax. Never stopped once to get his breath even. Hacked his way straight through the heart of the trunk and stood back to let her fall. A soldier has got rights above a citizen, I always says. Jupiter got himself changed to a white bull and goes out to a field where she is out to pick flowers. Takes his rights, too. Bellona, I recall now was her name. Her skirt in rags and on hinesides afore. Gave Jocelle a pretty mess of talk it's said."

Jocelle went out of the room suddenly, darting toward the hall and the foot of the stairs. The men were calling her back. Drake had called her.

"Jocelle!"

"Jocelle!"

"Here, Jocelle!"

"Jocelle!"

"Your granddad wants y'."

She came back within the door and closed it swiftly, to stand, her back to the door, her hand bent back to cover the shut latch. Drake was standing in his place. His hair hung in thin disheveled locks. He pushed the papers from beneath his fingers and rested his hands on the surface of the table, pushing the table forward. Standing thus he cried out:

"So help me God, I'll never set a foot on the green earth again."

"No, no," Jocelle cried out, "not for me. Not on my account. Don't say it."

"Jocelle, hear me while I say it. I'll never set my foot on God's green earth while time lasts for me." He leaned forward and beat the table with his right fist. "Let them take their damned-to-hell wars and famines and lifetimes, their say-so and religions and debts, their mortality, their resignations, their live and let live in one ear and out the other, so-help-me-God philosophies, continents that stick up out of the sea to make war on one another. Pot boys, two-forked, rape and rapine, Bellona-whip, Foch-Haig, submarine, Cavell, Liberty Bonds, influenza, Russia collapsed, Cambrai! So-help-me! Hear what I say. Jocelle! New covenant. I'll never set foot on earth again while time lasts."

VII

THE preparations for war had gone forward swiftly, winter and spring. The selected men had been gathered into the camps. Flags were displayed and national songs sung at all public gatherings. Portions of the army had gone overseas. A flag with a gold star hanging in a window indicated that an inmate of the house had been killed in service. The people were gathered into a rapt unit, assembled by dread and by devotion to the sacrificial youth. They were subdued and quiet under their distress. At a large county gathering in the town the people walked about the streets in a hushed fervor. The drafted men who had not yet been sent abroad came back to march before their families, this being their farewell. In the little towns there was, at such times, no cheering. As the men came, there was no sound above the soft tap of footsteps and the murmur of speaking voices until the musicians walked forward.

With the breaking of the winter Jocelle began to prepare for the growing of a chosen breed of fowl. She talked with Drake of this as they sat before the fire, as they studied pamphlets under the lamplight. Then Drake had built for her a large pen, enclosed with chicken-wire at the sides and overhead, a security from the hawks and crows. As a part of the enclosure he had erected a building to house the fowl in bad weather. The space at the top of the pasture was used for these new arrangements, the spot where once the swine had been butchered, and all the small pens there except one were destroyed to make way for this, the one left being that one, close behind the cabin, where the animals were brought for his scrutiny. Dickon built the neat houses for the fowl, muttering meanwhile of war, of war fowl, war debts, war diseases, chaos, unformed matter, building the structures carefully after the designs Jocelle furnished.

The chickens, white plymouth rocks, were hatching through April and May. They were strangely gentle creatures, bred in abundance and security. When the little ones began to feather, they grew dainty whorls of white about their "knees," and the same ornament was repeated more minutely at the back of the head and about the ears. If Jocelle leaned over their drinking pans or feeding bins, they would flutter to her shoulders and away, so that they were a continual flowing spray that drifted over her, their small pink feet tapping lightly on her hands or leaping over her arms. They were more appealing than the pigeons that took flight from the stable-yard, being more gentle and having but brief arcs of flight in which to move, as if their flight were designed for ornament rather than security. Two hundred white fowl, half-grown, making together a flock, hatched together, growing all in the same measure, they were, collectively, one personality or unit of being as they supplemented one another in their flights and demeanors, as they repeated the whorl of feathers about the legs, scarcely two being identical but all being of the same pattern. Seeing them as one, Jocelle fed them and sensed their eagerness to have the food, their creeping into the little hutches when the dark began to fall, their identical purring cries of twilight fear and assurance. When they were put away securely, she would leave them in the dusk, feeling that she had housed one creature, a gentle white monster, an entity that bore two hundred qualities or relations but brought all to its unified being.

J.T. had been called to the camp, and the younger of the Negro men was gone. Bob Terry, from beyond the front hill, assumed J.T.'s share in the partnership of the sheep. He would come and go among them, putting the lambs on the west pasture, guiding the mulatto boys in the shearing of the ewes. His loud, mellow voice would be pitched above the clamors of the stables:

"Carry the old eows out, now they're shorn. Ho, hooee! hooee! hoop! Shut fast the big gate. Open! Open! Keep back the buck-sheep!"

There was hearty noise and bluster among the sheep.

The voice that shouted orders would sometimes sing, scarcely waiting until Jocelle had left, if she went there with a message, to burst into a hearty song:

"Jerusalem, my happy home,
   Oh, how I long for thee . . ."

This was roared out with a great voice that delighted in the mellowed echoes that flowed around the broad o's in *home* and *long,* that in no moment seemed to long for anything beyond the moment's pleasure in tending the sheep, in rolling out a song before the middle stable wall. Laughter might follow, or interrupt any word, and the thundering "Carry out the eows! Keep back the old buck!" beat anywhere into the song.

In the bright early mornings Jocelle would fling out great handfuls of fine grain in the chicken-runs while the soft play of feathers fanned over her, and the flock, as one, swept forward to have the food. They would fly to the rim of her basket and swiftly away, or she would impose a wide arc of design upon the flowl by flinging out thus a handful of their crushed corn. She had a delight in the chickens that increased as they grew in beauty and deepened with her growing control over them. She made herself certain blue frocks to wear among them, and the waves of their soft white flutterings were a mist about the blue of her dress. With one of the mulatto boys to help she would grind the grain for their feedings at a hand-mill in the near stable. She studied a chart and prepared for them a balanced ration of protein and grain. Among them again, at feeding times, she laughed with the flutterings of their white wings and felt the soft wind of their flights at her throat and their sharp little pink feet on her shoulders.

With the passing of the spring she had become hearty, ripened with her delight in her fowl and with the warm sun. Her brown hair, when it was unbound, flew, clean and fine, in the drying air, and her frame became rounded and firm under the lightness of her movements. Deep of breast, her rounded arms moved among the chickens, and her trim form, clothed in a blue frock, stood waving corn over their flights and gathering or dispersing them. Her laughter ran above their low purring gratitude, or she flung up her head to answer the low summons of the horn that came from the bridge overhead. Waking at morning, she would remember first the fowl, and she would hurry through her tasks indoors and her care of Martha to be among them.

The long cry of the horn, Tobin wanted, and she would scarcely attend after the first blast made her know, by its length, that the anapæstic cry would not sound. More fowl had come to her pens. The first were sent away to the market after the second hatches were ready to take the runs, and thus the great white monster melted into the lesser entity of the new brood. Her motions were stayed and modified by the needs of the small chickens. Through

193

each act of mothering the new broods through the coming of their ornamental feathers and their more bold flights, she wished for Logan to be near her that he might see her fowl, that he might see here the unified flock, the collective, that he might feel with her the rush of their short flights and their brief resting on her arms and her shoulders. She would laugh with their fluttering, throwing up her head, her face to the sun.

She broke long sprays of yellow summer flowers to carry to Martha's room. "You're hearty as a milkmaid. Butter and curds in your skin. Red apples in your cheeks."

"I ate a yellow apple on the stairs."

"That tells the tale. Can swallow down an apple between the bottom and the top of a stair."

"What's the sign in't?"

"Hearty as a milkmaid. A deep-breasted, deep-hearted woman, Jocelle Drake, Juno when she stands against the mantel and holds the toasting fork, Aphrodite when she comes this way, toward me, with a twirling leaf in her fingers, her chariot drawn by white plymouth rocks for doves. The daughter of Dione, was it . . . ? and, say, Zeus. A cup of milk in her hands . . . Ate the apple on the stairs. Instead of throwing it, or who threw it, anyway, or did Paris, or how was it? 'For the most beautiful,' carved on the apple, and she ate it on the staircase. Saved a lot of trouble. Simply ate it and had done with it. Something about a girdle. Cincture, the famous zone. Whoever, that

is whatever woman, put it on, could have whatever man
she liked. One could borrow it when she wasn't using it.
Several borrowed it, but now she keeps it on all day, wears
it for herself."

She let Martha have her flight of laughter, and she made
only a smiling comment with grimaces and posings—the
milkmaid, skipping softly around the rug and singing
halfway under her breath:

"Where are you goen, my pretty maid?
. . . I . . . go a-milken, sir, she said . . ."

Whistling in a whisper, smiling down upon Martha,
who lay beside the window, she twirled an imaginary spray
of juniper or whatever pagan herb Martha asked for in
her banter. Martha asked then, singing:

"What is your fortune, my pretty maid?" ·

and her reply slowly sung:

"My father is a farmer, sir, she said.

"Tells the whole story. Good-by. I'm gone to grind
corn."

Logan came once, furtively. His car was left beyond the
pond, and he came toward the house in the dusk. He grew
dark with the gathering night. The chickens were housed
in their little hutches and the sun was gone, and thus she

had nothing to offer to dispel his darkness. Walking from the pond and back, he would be explaining his theories of human security, of ownership. He had been called to a camp in early summer. His future was uncertain.

His hair, which once had seemed bright, had darkened and was thin at the temples. His hands were nervous, making continual gestures of appeal and explanation. After his greeting he seemed to have forgotten Jocelle and to have forgotten his mission at Wolflick if he had come with any design clearly in view. He greeted her absently beside the pond, remembering later to kiss her cheek, rubbing his hands together, turning one palm uncertainly over the other, and stood in the roadway or walked up and down in a short space.

"At the bottom. It would have to begin at the bottom," he said in a rush of anger.

She joined him in the instant, agreeing to anything his mind might devise, wanting him then to have his wish, whatever it might be. She stood before him in the late glow of the sunset, flushed inwardly with her desire to serve him, to give him whatever he might need. In mind she flung herself into his arms, straightening his clenched hand to enclose herself, wanting to cry: "Have it, whatever it is, the Collective, the universal good, the farm-unit, the land-collective, the labor-general. Take it to keep." Thus she stood beside him, flushed by her constant inner wish.

196

"Oh, I wish you could have it so, whatever 'tis," she said.

He was nebulous and strange, sitting beside her on the stones at the edge of the water, his head against her breast, his hands holding the cloth of her garment. His eyes were closed as if he were sleeping, but he waked suddenly and kissed the folds that he held in his hands. He was beautiful in the coming moonlight, leaning thus, passive, upon her, holding the blue dress that was faintly blue now in the faint light. Sitting thus, she wondered about the moon and wondered what this strange presence was that leaned upon her, its eyes closed, its head against her, its lips parted, sleeping some strange sleep. Leaning forward she could barely touch his brow with her lips, but she kissed there whispering: "Have it, whatever 'tis."

He arose from his seat beside her and, taking her hands, raised her to her feet. He was elusive still, and nebulous, as half-defined, in this act; and, talking, they walked back to the porch and sat for a little while among the splotches of moonlight that had come to the grass. The warm twilight had passed into the warmth of the night. While he talked quietly, Jocelle became lost in grief and pity. Her voice would have told of her tears, and so she sat for a half-hour, quiet without but, from moment to moment, weeping within or growing calm with abstraction, the motions recurring until it seemed that the presence beside her had become a gaunt negation, a stark anger that had founded her in fresh sorrow and tears.

"How could you ever bring it about?" she said once, her voice scarcely heard, whispering calmly in some pause he had made. "It would take years. . . . No two would ever think alike. . . . Peace is the best. If we could have peace, then time would be to think out some good way, some better plan. . . ."

"Sit by and see men kill one another and don't know what they're killing for. See them come to ruin and no help for't." He finished speaking suddenly and stood before the pillar at the steps. His hands were beating together as at the beginning of the hour. He went quickly down the steps saying strangely: "Good night, Jocelle, good night, good-by. Until I see you again," spoken slowly, a word at a time, and he turned to walk swiftly away, toward the pond, toward the roadside gate, where he had left the conveyance that had brought him there.

When he was gone, she cried far into the night, seeking to bring coherence into his passionate greeting of her, his head upon her bosom, his absent-minded replies to her words of devotion, his walking away from the pond, his hard theories stated again as imperative redress, his strange departure. Morning came and she had slept but little. She went among the fowl, dreary and restless, or she took corn from the cornroom in the farther stable and made a show to herself of getting it ground, being listless and troubled.

"What did he mean, or what did he come to?" she asked herself, being overcome by his chaotic trouble, his vague absence, his lengthy dissertations, his thought of himself as one to redress the earth's ills, his raptures over theories of human life and good. Anger came slowly to her. He might have given her a more clear farewell. He would be going to a camp, perhaps for detention. He did not make himself known to her.

Martha did not know of the secret visit, and thus no mention of Logan was made. The pleasantry continued above stairs. She seemed gay with the summer, hectic with the passage of the troops overseas. All around was the teeming season and the abundance of the fields and the pastures. The chickens grew swiftly and were sent away, sold to the traders, but others came swiftly in their places and there was no lack of fluttering white birds about Jocelle's shoulders. Thinking that Logan might have made his distress more clear to her, that he might have given her a share in it, her anger spread to envelop all her thought of him. She determined that she would have no more storms or scenes within. She would, she determined, move among candors and clear-seeing.

She resolved that she would think of him no more. He might fold his troubled hands into the folded sheets of paper on which he had written, fold himself entirely thus into an envelope and label it Farm-Collective or whatever he devised. She determined that she would not lose her hearty health for him nor sink into a distress that would maim her body. She kept much among the open fields and the sunny runs of the fowl, and she ate well of the rich foods that were brought to the board. "Once is enough," she said, remembering her shrunken form and tightened life after the previous summer. She drank cream and milk in the kitchen and went back to her work among the fowl. In an act of denial which she wished to make final, as if she would sweep her heart clean, she resolved to destroy the documents left in her care, to burn these tight-written theories and counter-plans and to house no more of them. He had made of her a repository of smudgy paper written over with ink, cramped with marginal after-thoughts which were themselves revised and further annotated. Did he think he had gained her affection and her fervid devotion? She shed his dry, excited theories of a social being, a new man, a new day, thrusting all care of them from her thought. Anger increased. She would have no more of him, she resolved, of this no-man, this theory-monger, lost in his fog.

She saw him going into the distances into which he had merged, his long limbs walking swiftly, his shape distantly seen as moving arms and legs retreating further. Body and mind, he was gone. About her lay a nothingness of distorted objects and wrong-headed purposes, the war in her own chicken pen gathering the war-chickens into crates to send them away. Inside the house was wrong-headedness again, letters that told her nothing but the little that was conveyed to her passion from the handwriting that made the dissertation with cramped and hurried strokes of pencil or pen. Even these bulky envelopes which she had read from the outside, from the sweeping strokes of the first pages to the harried and minute intricacies of the rest, came now no more. He had gone dry even of theory. He had made of her a moldy vault into which he had locked whatever drear opinions played into his mind from whoever came, or of Joel Hagan, or of himself. Promiscuity and smelly foul words mouthed over by fifty men; she would burn them all and forget them. She would carry all to the garden beyond the growing plants, where the ashes were dumped into a little pit, and she would burn them there.

When this determination settled upon her, she felt an ease, as if she had cleansed her thought of distress. She would burn all and forget them. The resolve to put the papers from her, to obliterate them, was so strong and so final that the act of destruction remained unaccomplished and unremembered.

At the roadside letter box she would fold the letters out of her sight within a bent newspaper, and she would walk, unknowing, ignoring, back across the pasture through the late-summer avenue that was smudged with quick-grass that came the day after a warm rain, that withered in three days of sun. Her passionate precaution was unnecessary, for, when Martha laid out the letters on her bed and put those for Drake together, there was nothing from Logan. Jocelle was frequently wanted at the bridge or in the room below where Drake planned the coming year and made notes or wrote orders.

"She's as ruddy as a rose," Martha said to her.

"The wind reddens me, now since August is here."

"It is true . . . ? Is it true . . . ?" Martha would be asking something. "Do men find greater opportunity for individualism when they are lost in the general mass . . . greater than when they are trapped in family life? . . ." Calling later from the window when Jocelle set forth for the letter box to carry Drake's orders: "Put a red ribbon on your hair!" or: "Wear the scarf with the rose border!" Back from the mailbox, empty-handed, she would hear the thresher beating its even throb through the farm, the men in the field back of the stable pasture threshing the wheat.

The wheat stood first for three days until the straw was baled into bundles. Drake shouted orders from the bridge. The laden wagons, piled with sacks of grain, passed in review before the man at the lookout, and each wagon was written upon the sheet of a book. Jocelle was sent to take samples of the grain from three sacks. She brought the grain to the bridge, and when it was inspected, she flung it widely into the enclosure below, where the common fowl of the barn were running, and they leaped forward, their wings and beaks outspread. Walking far on the hill-side to the west, where the sheep and lambs had fed in the spring, where the sheep now grazed with the beef calves, the hoarse anapæst from the horn brought her back, herself put anew into the throat of the bugle.

One day, as she passed inside at the doorway from the pantry, Drake stood before the cabinet of the guns which he had opened. He held in his hand a curious iron object that was rusted brown. He held it out toward her briefly and looked at her above the smoke of the pipe which he held in his mouth.

"A lantern," he said.

It was of an octagonal shape, the sides that cut away the corners being shorter than the faces. The top sloped to a cone, and at the point an iron ring was fixed. He opened the door and inside were sockets for three candles, one of them partly broken. The rust was brown over all of it, and the four sides that made the faces were perforated with ornamental design which would let out the light.

"I recollect, when I was a boy, it used to be around," he said. "A lantern. Used in Fort Harrod when the Ainsleys came, and with them the Coopers and the Glovers. Common men, they were, who did an uncommon thing."

He had dusted it with a napkin. It was sturdy and only the one candle socket was broken, but the door would not shut completely because of the rust. "Scour away the iron-rust, and it'll shut true," he said, bending over it. He gave it suddenly into her hands and he looked upon her admiringly as she turned it about. "Carried it when they went outside at night, or hung it out to light a friend home." He took the pipe from his mouth and laid it on the ledge of the cabinet. She knew that he had some purpose in showing her the relic. His face was thin and strong, heavy under its finely cut lines. His mouth was moist from the use of the pipe, and his lips were flexible, bending slightly without words as he looked at the lantern which she now held against the ledge beside the pipe, for it was heavy. A tenderness as of a mother-feeling came over her as she saw him thus, and she remembered that he had renewed his vow for her. He was trying to say something more by the way of the lantern.

"You can keep it," he said.

"I didn't know about it," she replied, and she thanked him for the gift. "How did I never hear about it?"

"It got to be something to keep a long time after it wasn't used up for scrap-iron," he said, smiling, and he took back the pipe to his mouth.

She would take care of it, she said. It might hang somewhere in the hall, to be taken out to the hook beside the outer door if light were wanted outside. She would find some candles to burn in it, or she might find a little oil lamp that would set inside. He took it into his hands again and showed her how it was made. His ancestor, a smith, had made it. John Glover had been a blacksmith when such craftsmen made things. Glover had made plows, traps for hunting down the animals, andirons to hold up the fire, knives and spears and chains. He had made the lantern. He had punched out the perforations to make the design, the holes that let out the light.

She looked again at the designs and saw that no two sides were exactly alike, and saw the irregular regularities where balance was made again and again. She laughed softly over it, wanting to run with it to Martha's room, but scarcely daring to take any part of the occasion for her own, letting him give it slowly to her again, and he said again that it was hers. He locked the cabinet and went briskly up the stairs. Outside were the busy days, the mailbox under the beech tree, the return to Martha's room. Beyond, farther, and the armies were rolling up victories and thrusting forward for the last great encounter on all fronts. "What has happened to the world?" Martha cried out to her, in terror, her prophecies of diplomatic adjustments having failed. The wild crab-grass had spread over the fields, a late growth that came if the season were wet. In Martha's room the seeds of this untended wild grass dropped from her shoes and were dusted from her clothing.

"Will it be, will it be that men will always look to some overlying power, the Government, to find them jobs, to find them opportunities for labor? means? living? Will they cease to create for themselves?" Martha questioning, a cup of milk held to her thin lips.

"The New World."

"Yes. Tell Elkins, Wade, whatever-his-name, not to forget my fire again." She would be wretched, cold under the wool comforters, in bed before the open window.

Jocelle was sorry because of the forgotten fire and she went to find the coal herself. She made the flame come again to the grate while the Lenin Revolution, begun the November before, engaged the sick woman. Her bed was strewn with journals, and Logan appeared again, in her frequent questioning. "Will there be no more wars, Jocelle? Would you like to live in a beehive and be a bee? And which bee would you be, if you could be a bee?"

In late September news came of the death of Walter. He had been killed during August in a trench street. After this report spread over the farm, quiet followed. Drake went up and down the stairs but he called no orders from the bridge, and later he sat staring at the cabinet to the left of his fireplace. Martha cried, wringing her hands together, and she fumbled among the newspapers to try to find reports dating back to the offensive movements of early August, trying to place Watler again in battle through the brief paragraphs that told of action and sector and advance.

Jocelle fed her war-fowl through the shock of the foreign message, morning and noon and evening, and their short arcs of flight and their eagerness to have the grain could not delight her, they having become a part now of the strangeness that had come to the farm, evil and good being mingled and opposed, being continually in opposition even while they were intertwined and entangled. Dry-eyed, she fed the fowl, pained by the message that made of Walter a heroic being. She saw him thundering down a trench street; she wanted to hate him anew, having thus remembered him, for he had been in part forgotten. Justice had been given her but she could not discern it clearly. An unworded and unconscious wish had all the while clung about her knowledge of his danger; she had wanted him not to return; had wanted never to see him again. But she had not devised death for him.

Days passed. The war had rolled near again in this last distress. Martha spoke of him tenderly and cried in the telling of places he had been, tracing his probable course over a map of France. "Walter is dead," she said to Jocelle, searching her face for the emotion that might follow the renewed report. "He was killed in battle," she said.

"I know."

"Did you ever kill him in your thought?"

"I do not think so," Jocelle cried out. "I am sure I never." Martha cried back to her, beating her hands together:

"I burned the house down over *his* head. Everybody else gone. Nobody but Drake in it. I burned it down. It was about the time the deafness left me. Day after day I burned it down."

"Don't remember it now," Jocelle said. "Don't remember . . ."

"You did not kill?"

"Oh, no, I did not. Never, I think."

The dead man made of Logan an even more nebulous unreality. The real was at hand. She remembered the real with forgiveness and pity. When she had fed her fowl many times, evening and morning, when she had walked to the mailbox day after day to get the journals, or when she had turned the hand-mill in the barn to grind the grain for the chickens, no personal message having come from Logan, no message of any sort, whether theory or plan, a conviction grew upon her that she should put himself and her troubled love out of her mind by substituting some other.

"Came to me out of the foot-rot of the sheep. . . . Out of the sour old ewe sick on the stable floor . . ." She would remember him standing before her on a January morning before the stable, Martha beside her on the bench. His smile would be near her then, his head lowered to the level of her shoulder while he listened to what she said. The picture mingled with her anger. She appraised him as misguided, unjust, ill-balanced, rude, self-fixed, and wanting in the tenderness a man gives to a woman. He was without manly being. "Came to me out of the rot of the stables," she cried out of a dream. Finding she could not hush her arguments and stay the continual contentions within her, she resolved to fasten her mind elsewhere. When this notion seized her, she dwelled upon it frequently, approaching it as a refuge. She would, she decided, put herself in the way of another affection. It was outrageous that the death of Walter should haunt her, recurring, and give her a confusion of hatred and glorying forgiveness and self-accusation. Logan should be filling her mind and consoling her distress. She would, she determined, fill her mind with another being and shut out this dour entanglement that yielded her recurring pain. Having tried again and again to remove the troubled relations from herself and to fortify her being against the distresses that attended her, she would, she contrived, order her life otherwise.

"I'll save out what's wanted and smother the rest," she said. "You can't tear it out. There's always a root left back that grows big in a few minutes. Fasten it on another. That's the only way. The thing's mine anyway, whatever it is."

The war had gone sour on itself, she concluded, watching sadly as her war-chickens fluttered to their food. Stump, the Negro boy, sang in the cornfield toward the creek while he cut the corn, this distant shouting being the last delight left to the fields as they lay sloping gently away from the chicken pens and were seen over the fluttering white of the fowl. The afternoons would be quiet while Stump rested from his song, but he sang again at the quitting time when the chill of the early dark would be falling. Or Bob Terry came frequently to talk with Drake through the months of the autumn. He would come knocking at the west door of the diningroom and sit on the porch there. His hands would finger slips of paper, his memoranda of the sheep, for he had come to ask an advance or a loan of a small sum of money. If he seemed boisterous, breaking the afternoon with his shouting in his first appearance, she saw presently the neatness in his hearty skin that was pink and clean. His hat would rest on the floor behind his chair. Sometimes his two small children would come with him, and then Jocelle would take them to see her white fowl, if these were still in the runs, or she would give them little cakes in the kitchen. The men would be talking:

"It'll end in a year or less," Drake said. "It can't last now."

The prices of land would be quoted, the rapid rise of values, the sales of farms here and there. "If I had a few thousand ahead I could . . ."

"Better hold fast to what you've got," Drake said.

They would be speculating, making prophecies:

"Say prices hold up another year . . ."

It was idle talk in the west doorway. Drake cared little for what was said of the war, confusing the names of the generals and placing them in scornful mock-ignorance on the wrong sides. Chessmen, dropped from the board, he set them back anywhere, right side up or down.

Terry seemed outspoken to her as he sat beyond Drake, his chair on the gravel just off the porch. He would arise and walk toward the doorway, over the porch or back to the gravel, yielding continually to the sand, to the boards, to the chair again, and he was free in his movements as he stepped with light-heavy tread. He would laugh through his speaking, and he would look toward her with amused comment in the soft purr of his laughter that said to her: "Am I right?" Back toward the barns and the pasture, he would be managing the ewes, getting them to autumn pasture and seeing them warmly housed at evening if rain threatened. He would be mounting his brown mare at the stable door and ride away home out the avenue and over the south hill. Back again, on another day, his voice shouting to Drake from without, he flowed with the air and stumbled with his half-stumbled step at the threshold to come inside and ask for a record of the old ram, his age and pedigree. His wants seemed simple and easily stated. His skin was soft with a constant bath of sweat. He would be beautiful in secret before Martha's accounts of armies rolling up victories along the Meuse and in the Argonne, each account of fluttering victories predicting the end of wars and the return of soldiers, or "Walter is dead," Martha called after her as she went down the stair. "War-bride, war-witch, war-widow," was implied in the threatened taunt. Jocelle kept among the chickens and the turkeys and let the clear sun of autumn redden her face and her throat.

"The Germans have offered to negotiate peace," Martha spoke softly from her window, her voice among the upper boughs of the trees as a flat bird-call or the hollow drumming of some feeble woodpecker that urged hurry upon her or threatened her decision.

Terry came to the garden under the walnut tree where she had swung his two little sunburnt girls. The late bees were gathering about a few left, ungathered grapes, and innumerable small gnats were sucking the soured juices through the thin withering hulls, the leaves dried and falling. She was taking dried butterbeans from their hulls.

He was gallant, bending over her hand, over her lap. She was glad that he had come in his everyday guise—courtly bow, blue gingham shirt, rough brogans. She liked him then as the gallant plowman. His teeth were even and fine, pearl-clear and strong. His hands were soft on her hands. His eyes darted forth beams of light, the brightness of an admiring eye. His face had been clean-shaven that day, in her honor she conjectured.

When he had kissed her, she began to talk to him of Logan, to whom, she said, she was betrothed. He was con-

fused and angry, and he called her a vixen. She saw herself
then as, perhaps, a vixen, and her blurred thought made
her smile while she looked down at the dry pods of the
beans, or she tried to assume again her admiration of him
and glanced upward to see again his blue eyes. But he
changed ground, becoming a wronged man, confused between anger and shame. She left the garden suddenly,
having no argument, and she went to the parlor where she
played a little on the piano while he stood outside behind
the chimney.

He came inside presently and stood by the piano while
she played irregular repetitions in waltz time, setting him
apart, drawing a line beyond which his understanding
could not reach.

"But he's gone, ain't he? He's in prison, ain't he now?
What good ever will a man do you in prison?"

He was, perhaps, in detention, she said. The presence of
this one made the other more actual. She looked at the
near face suddenly and saw the hidden and absent one.
As he talked and as she played, she thought that she had
lost the other one in geometric lines, in some pattern of
what she supposed he should be in this circumstance or
that. The near flesh brought back to her the other, and
brought the ways of a mouth in speaking, in smiling, in
waiting for her reply. Bringing again, it brought back
the ambitions or needs of a heart, a spirit within flesh
crying out by the way of words and eyes and trusting de-

votions. A joy in loyalty welled up within her. Delight rushed through her and she smiled to say: "John Logan Treer is a good man. I was confused, addled, I guess. He'll come back when the war's over. And Martha says it's nearly done. Austria is about to draw out of it. Forty-two American divisions in France. It's almost over. He'll come back. I want him to come."

Where the bright leaves fell from the autumn trees, they lay on the ground, making a variegated carpet that reflected what color had passed over the trees, for crimson lay under the oaks and orange russet under the sugar maples. The Austrian army had been split in two, and an armistice had been sought, signed early in November. On November sixth a gale blew, and the leaves were swept through the air to lodge withered and bruised and packed among distant bushes or fence-corners, and where they had lain the ground was burnt by the frost until it lay shadowed in browns and withered of its grass. Johnnie Briggs came back from his long sojourn, giving no account of his absence. He came weeping in at the kitchen door, saying that he had been amiss of his duty, and he sat weeping beside the kitchen fire until he was asked to come within. The hair had grown back on his face. Later he said that he had suffered the pestilence that was sweeping the country as a backwash from the war. He had lain ill of it three weeks, and strength then had come back to him slowly. His prayer was again in the house: "Seedtime and harvest, and cold and heat, and summer and winter, and day and night shall not cease . . ."

German delegates were reported as leaving Berlin to treat for an armistice. Martha called frequently from the upper room, or she called after the physician as he went down the stairs, summarizing the end. Word of the signing of the armistice on November eleventh came with the coming of the doctor, whose visit fell that day. Her ear to the telephone, Jocelle heard the cheering in the town, where the people had assembled without plan or program in the square, the distant ringing of the courthouse bell and the church bells brought by some accidental telephone connection. Raptures of delight and sadness moved each one to forget his habitual tasks and pleasures. Jocelle sat with Martha in the firelight or she walked back through the fields in a wild midnight wind. Asking if the war would be over in truth, if it could really have come to an end, she went across the first pasture, beyond the place where her war-chickens had been housed. The stars were bright and abundant in the sky. The wind blew without clouds, and the half-moon stood still beyond the reach of the fitful bluster that whirled leaves and bent the grass. What would it be for the war to cease? she asked, having for so long a time been pitched to the fervor of war.

Back, and in the quiet of the late morning, she read a

part of Logan's papers, the undestroyed documents that had not left her chest. Wanting to discover him beneath the writing, she read swiftly, looking for his mind under the theories of ownership, of communal relations. Into this reading a message came from him, brought from the letter box by Tobin. He would be at Wolflick in two months, he thought, and the time seemed long to her as she lived it, looking forward. Wrapped in an old cloak and a head-shawl she flung corn to the great full-grown turkeys in the pen behind the middle stable, and it seemed to her then, viewing the two months, viewing the three-ply theory she had derived from the closely written papers in her chest, that Logan was passive in love, that he had from the beginning waited to be chosen, selected, taken by herself to her choice, and that he dealt in mysteries for all his clear statements, and she laughed, coming from the barn, and smiled again and again as she went to the cellar for apples and picked over the bins there to take away the spoiling fruit.

"What is it?" Martha asked her.

"Logan. He'll come in six weeks or so."

She kept her counsel within herself, replying to nothing more, keeping laughter and argument, pleasantness and inquiry. An argument to end all arguments, and she weighed her wish and her confusion against remembered pictures of him, of his unconscious sweetness in a certain

216

June when he had told her what blight ailed a little apple
tree.

He, what was he, she asked herself, Logan Treer? She
did not want to ask Martha now. She wanted to know him
for herself and in her own knowledge. *Logan* placed him
on one side among the old forted towns of the pioneers.
He was large, as she remembered him beside a door, tall
but so evenly proportioned that he would be thought of
as in the average build unless one measurement were taken
alone. A straight, sharply defined nose, the *Treer* of him
perhaps, whatever that might be. He was visionary, mili-
tant, melancholy in his concern for mankind and in his
thought of himself as being mankind. He was elusive, not
to be analyzed, to be comprehended in a mass rather, or
left as the source of wonder or surprise. She remembered
his paternal feeling toward the people of the farms. As
an indefinite sweetness beside her that gave warmth to
her arguments he existed, rather than as a clearly remembered picture or a sum of remembered details. She could
not wholly recall how he looked even when, surprising
herself, she would reproduce his sudden step at the west
doorway or his tall body crumpled in Martha's chair. The
remembered view, when she sat beneath his horizontal
and saw thus the long teeth downward pointing, did not
disturb the sum of his being as it accompanied her own
identity, and she went far across the farm to the large

217

hickory trees and gathered three bushels of fine nuts into sacks which Tobin later brought to the barn in a wagon. Sitting in her own room, the west room above, she sewed for herself a fine wool dress of a rich, dark burnt-umber shade, and she pressed flat each seam and stitched a silk thread of decoration flatly into the cloth, and wove with her fingers a braided belt of silken cord.

"With your brown cloak," Martha said.

An undefined preparation was thus faintly admitted between them. The armistice had been celebrated from city to city throughout the conquering world. An army of occupation had moved into the valley of the Rhine. Jocelle's thought was sweetened by a will to leave armies and treaties and international blunderings and predictions of after-war disasters, and to make, here, an order, a peace, through her own person set to rights, and to make comfort and pleasure for the other one. His second letter, a letter of passion and endearments, named more exactly the day of his coming, but she, remembering Martha's coming lover of the years past, kept her secret, sharing with none at Wolflick, although this letter blinded her eyes and quickened her breath so that she was unable to read all of it understandingly for an hour, remembering Martha again in this distress but telling nothing. Writing in answer she flung out a midnight missive which included a bit of the umber cloth, saying that this fragment was of her wedding gown. She ran with this swiftly sealed letter to the mailbox after midnight through a blundering rain that muddied the driveway and confused the path, and all through the remainder of the night, while she slept and waked, she remembered that the mail-carrier did not come until near eleven o'clock in the morning, that she could yet go back to the box and retrieve the letter, but she did not.

A raw night in the late winter, and outside a light fog had settled down from the enclosing hills and made a white glimmer about the moon. Jocelle, dressed in the umber dress, waited in the parlor, expecting to hear the throb of the motor that would bring Logan to Wolflick. The house seemed quiet, as if it awaited the early bedtime and the covering of the fires. Stoner Drake sat before his hearth with Sol Dickon and Jack Briggs, for Briggs had come that day from Gritty Creek. Hearing the low summons on the horn, Jocelle went back through the hall and into the half-opened door of the diningroom.

"I see fire in the east room," Drake said to her. "Who comes here tonight? Who told Stump to build more fire there?"

"I told him to bring the coal and wood. I built it there myself."

"You're a young thing." The mouth drawn down as if it would say: "A young thing for a hussy."

"I am twenty-three," quietly spoken.

219

"Who is it?"

"It's John Logan Treer. I'm not afraid to call a name."

"The bean beetle. The registered shorthorn. The stomach worm in the stomach of the Supreme Sheep. The big tapeworm. . . . The Phosphate Philoctetes. Cæsar among the cabbages. . . . The Species Man. The Collective Almighty. The grand Bull Durham. What time does he come here?"

"When I hear his car I'll know he's here. I've got no other way. The road will be heavy, mud and water."

In the parlor she mended the fire to a great flame and opened wide the shades of the windows to let out the light. Dickon came to the door, dragging his feet along the hallway. He came near to her as she stood near the middle of the room and he leaned above her to speak. His face near, his voice seemed to come from beyond his rough eyebrows that were tangled and intergrown, gray and black, curled and twisted as if the hairs were matted together, and she thought on the instant of the tangled jungles of wild growth near the creek and the obliterated burnt place there. She flung up her head to the light of the fire and looked at him, unafraid.

"Did you read my *Cosmograph?*" he asked.

"I read it. I skipped only a small part."

"Figurability? Retention? The Origin of Man?"

"I read to the end."

"First there was Chaos, unformed matter . . ."

"In it all the seeds of nature," she recited.

"In it was rudimentary thought, vegetation, all in in-cipiency. Order, Succession—one thing after another, that is. Thought, Night, Terra, a world, and what we call Love. You understand?"

"A part, I understand." Her head was still lifted, look-ing at him. She had stepped away two paces to be nearer the fire.

"Asleep, you might say, back of Providence. In in-cipiency. Back of all was Intention and Aptitude."

"Intention . . . Yes."

"And Aptitude. Apt to act in a certain way, that is."

"I won't care, Intention or Aptitude or what-not, if Logan cannot come here, now and always."

"Don't forget, though, what I've told y'."

"If he can't come here I'll burn up the *Cosmograph*. One hour! What's one hour?"

Martha's voice was calling from above. "Don't listen to talk, Jocelle. Don't let anybody tell you anything."

Dickon did not hear the words from above although he knew that someone had spoken. He called out louder:

"Chaos produced Earth, Love, Erebus, Night, and the Universe. Void space, that is. Earth comes first, though. The broad-breasted Earth they called 'er, like she was a wench. Mankind comes a long way down."

A loud blast of the horn went through the house. Jocelle hurried back to meet the anapæstic cry where it summoned her within the diningroom door. Dickon walked beside her, speaking in time with his hurried step that dragged and thumped beside her down the hall.

"Ne'er a one of all I've named y' cared the twit of a finger what came to a man or a woman or a beast," he said, speaking roughly into her ear. His black and gray hair stood stiff and heavy above his coarse brows and was a part now of the stick stubble above his sharp eyes. "Ne'er a one."

Briggs was speaking within the farther room. "I went past Fairhope Church today and I said: 'Oh, could I see Jesus again!' Once I saw Jesus . . ."

"One hour he can stay. The bean-beetle collective, the Species Man," Drake called out to her as she came within the door. "Mind well what I say. One hour."

Briggs began to speak, continuing, as if he had already begun his story. " 'Twas when I was a drinken man, my body steeped in sin. I went past a church on a hot summer day, bone-idle with laziness because my drink was in a way to go out of my head and leave me empty. I went inside Fairhope Church to ease me outen the heat of the day. Night before I'd been there with Amos Nick and a woman, his woman and mine, to drink on the doorstep.

"I went past Fairhope Church and I says: 'I wonder if inside I might find ease from the heat and the pain inside my head. I'll lay me down on a bench in the cool dark place and hear the grasshoppers outside in the graveyard.

Surely to goodness I can rest here,' I says. Sometime I'll tell all, how I heard Jesus say: 'Open the Book!' And I opened, and it was Genesis, and I learned from a learned man it means the Beginning."

Dickon began to speak when the other ceased. "Hera, the atmosphere that surrounds the earth. There you've got the source of all vegetative life. Ethereal seed, life for the planet. Productive principles. You've got Hera and Zeus. Sluttish stories to tell all the truth. Comes a long way down, mankind does. Hardly thought about. Almost got left out. Hah, hah, hah! Cools off your heat to know what a minute particle mankind—all in a bunch—is in front of all these causes. Death, then old Mors, dark wings. She comes to thunder at the door. Hunts down her prey."

Briggs spoke absently, as if he did not answer the other. "Genesis means how it began. God remembered Noah and every living thing . . . 'Open the Book!' and I read there, forward and back . . ."

The sound of the motor car began to be heard. It was coming over the drive beyond the pond, coming swiftly nearer. The voices were hurrying, speaking together:

"One hour he can stay. You hear me? See't he stays one only hour. One."

"Like I said, incipient in Chaos . . ."

"One hour. Mark well the timepiece."

"Jocelle!" A scream from above.

"Who's up there?" called out.

223

"If he can't come where you are, you blow hell straight through Chaos. God! Jocelle, don't let anybody tell you . . ."

"Who is she, up there?" Dickon asked, listening.

"It's Francesca," the voice from above hissed in whispering, sobbing. "Don't let anybody talk . . ."

The voices were rough in argument and long-sounding in loud dispute and speculation. Voices flowed through the house. Thus, thus, natural laws, defiance, or Hebraic relation of man to his God. Each argument was heightened by the coming lover, each man striving to state himself anew.

Logan Treer came to the door. His knock was quick, devised to sound above the arguments inside the house. The voices were stilled while Jocelle went to open for him, but a low admonition came from above in a long whispered sign. She went across the hallway to the door, the voices behind her being quiet, and she pulled at the large door and felt it sway stubbornly in the casing. Then a strong blow was applied from without, another pressure put steadily upon it from above, and Logan came within, shutting back the mist and the frost.

Within the door he greeted her again and again, and he led her to the fire, flinging his outer coat aside. He looked at her with delight, as if he rode to her upon some swift carrier, as if he were still riding. "How lovely she is," he said. "I had not remembered half."

"Oh, the war, the war, is it over?" she asked.

"No, it's not over," he answered, but he lost none of his delight, and he caught her again to his arms. The loud arguments flowed anew before the other fire, and their words fell to whisperings. He had brought the marriage license, he said, and he took it from his coat, but it was soon forgotten on the table, as if it had been already served and satisfied. Then Drake walked through the house to the parlor and stopped a short distance within the door. Logan came forward to greet him, but he was stayed.

"One hour." The hand was lifted, forbidding. "One hour. Mind what I say. He can never stay here more. Married or single, bound or free, one hour. The Species Man. The Man-General. He'll know what it is to be the Species Man. The begetter of the race. One hour."

He left as soon as he had spoken. They stood apart before the fire looking at each other with surprise that continually melted into renewed delight and continually appeared again. He drew forward a chair for her and he sat beside her on another or he stood before her. She was afraid, but not of him, and she sat before him as a hearty presence from the fields come indoors. She told him again and again that he was the same that she had remembered from the beginning, that she had lost his clear image for a little, but she corrected this statement suddenly and cried out:

"I lost you for a long while. It was the war took me."

He seemed to be leaping on the hearth-rug. He stood quietly looking down upon her, saying that she was lovely, that her smile was a sprite that bent her thin red mouth from the even strand of her glittering teeth, and he laid his hand lightly on the sleeve of her dress that glowed with a rich light where the firelight throbbed through the mesh of the cloth and lit it to a pulsing crimson. The voice above, in a spent whisper, over the banister, called: "Don't delay, Jocelle. Do whatever is to do," but he did not hear beyond her own speaking. "The war took me, away, or somehow, took me."

Looking past the differences that had passed, looking at the year just gone, looking to see the constant figure of her passions, she told him again and again that she was the same, that she had never really changed. There would be a good deal to tell when there was time, she said again, crying out: "The war, is it over? When will it be over?"

"We won't care, war or not, outside or in, if we love together."

He sat beside her, and he began to tell her of what had happened in the months past, saying there was not time now to tell. He made a hurried report of passages from one place to another, of injustice, of harried surmises, of personal ambitions and political blunderings and the kindness of friends. He had not wanted her to know of the

humiliations and degradations put upon him. He had
been hissed in a public square. He might not be able to
find a place to work, employment, for a long time, for he
had been despised as a slacker, as one outside the vast
group and classed with the enemy. He was outside, he supposed, but, he cried out suddenly: "I ought not to have
been. They'll see it after awhile. I was inside. I was at the
very heart of the age, at the beginning of what's to come
after." She leaped up suddenly, as if she were ready for
flight, and she caught both his hands, smiling and drawing him. He stood beside her on the hearth, holding her
arms, and they were both then ready for swift departure,
caught in a pose of flight. He smiled with her then, and
he said: "What will we do? what will we do?"

She had not lost her delight and she murmured that
she could not stay away from Wolflick long, that she must
care for Martha, and he agreed to this, murmuring
Martha's name between his caresses.

"We must make some plan now," he said.

"Oh, we must."

"Whatever comes, we can take it somehow."

Then she asked him if he knew Martha's story, and he
said that he did, that she had told him enough for him to
guess the rest. She cried out suddenly that they would go
away together and find some quiet, untroubled place,
some place whose war story was not their own story, and

he caught her more deeply to himself and agreed to this, but he said that such a place would be, for him, hard to find.

They were sitting again, speaking quietly, looking into the glow of the fire. "They talk about the unknown soldier," he said, "and the *unknowing* soldier he was, rather, out to kill and get killed to make fifty rich men richer. Oh, God pity us. I always held no man could make more than a million dollars in a lifetime and make it honestly, but here, of late, men, a few men, made a million in one year, and made it off this blinding, tear-gassed, shell-shocked wretchedness that ruined us, ruined Walter and is bound to ruin John Thomas and Ben and Sam and Joel Hagan and Charlie and Terry and Hood and any you'll name."

A sudden cry from above aroused them from these contemplations, a warning. Martha was calling from above in a half-spent whisper: "Jocelle, Jocelle, twenty minutes is all left."

They went to the other room, and when Logan had spoken to each man there, Jocelle made known her intention. None offered to dispute her plan. She walked among them, her head lifted. "It will be in Martha's room," she said, "and any who wants to come had better go there now." She was swift, making only a few explanations. "Preacher Briggs can say the ceremony." Logan reminded all that two witnesses would be necessary to sign the paper. Briggs settled his clothing to a neater order and he put on his shoes. He went to the cabin and brought Mrs. Tobin. "For a witness," he said. Drake offered no comment. He seemed scarcely to notice what passed, but sat, his head lowered, as if he were in some partial coma or trance. Jocelle touched his shoulder lightly in passing, reaching with her finger, but she made no further effort to arouse him. She went then to Martha's room, doing all swiftly, and she told Martha what would follow. Dickon did not come up the stairs. Standing with her hands clasped in those of her lover, she heard the brief ceremony Briggs spoke before them, and afterward he prayed his accustomed prayer: "While the earth remaineth . . ."

When his amen had sounded slowly, as if it were sung with fervor after the promises of food and the tokens of supremacy which man might have above the beasts, Jocelle took the cloak and hat which Martha had made ready for her and she put them on swiftly. A little hand-bag filled with clothing stood near the door, prepared by Martha in the hour. Crying a swift good-by to all in the house, waving her hand to Martha in gratitude, she went with Logan through the hall and out the door, into the vague mist that had now obliterated the trees.

VIII

DRAKE aroused when Briggs came noisily down the stairs. A loud blast on the horn called after Jocelle, but no one answered this with comment. Then Dickon began to speak, as if he had been speaking, as if the coming of Briggs had interrupted him.

"Chaos produced Earth. Void space, that is. Unformed matter. In it nature, succession, and thought, human thought. In it Earth, Terra, they called her by a Latin name. All in incipiency. All back of Providence. 'Let 'er go,' was said, and off she goes, all the wheels a-turnen. Nobody cares as much as the spit out of your mouth what goes with any part of it."

The blow blast of the horn answered him, calling Jocelle again. Dickon let the sound pass before he took up his argument. "Hera, the atmosphere that surrounds the earth . . ." But here Briggs broke upon him in a loud voice, out-speaking his contention.

"Your blasphemy is unknown to me. I never saw words like yours in any book. God shut Noah inside the ark. God

shut the door. 'Preach where the book falls open,' he said
to me, and I read, forward and back from one line . . ."

"I wish Jesus would tell you again to open. You about
wore that place out. Maybe if you'd get drunk again, you'd
get a new place in the Book . . ."

"Leave Briggs be," Drake spoke up suddenly, his hands
tight on the arms of his chair.

"Forward and back, from one line that said: 'Seedtime
and harvest, and cold and heat, and summer and winter,
and day and night shall not cease.' . . . 'While the earth
remaineth,' you read, back of the line . . ."

"Cared not so much as the dirty rag on a sore finger
what went with any part. Obeyed what he had to do. His
insides worked toward the outside. Came out in action.
Didn't have one breath to say yea or nay," Dickon called
out, but Briggs spoke as if he addressed a gathering and he
ignored the interruption:

" 'Twas when I was a drinken man, my body steeped in
sin. I came past Fairhope Church on a hot day in a summer, bone-idle with laziness, and the drink on the way to
go outen my head and leave me empty. I went inside Fairhope Church to ease me outen the heat of the day. Night
before I'd been there with two more to drink and curse on
the doorstep, one Amos Nick and one a woman.

"I went past Fairhope and I say: 'If inside I might find
ease from the heat and the pain inside my head . . . I'll
lay me down on a bench in the cool dark place and hear

the grasshoppers outside in the graveyard. What's a church but a house?' Inside, I went then, and there 'twas. So still you'd hear a pin drop here or a creak of sound there, off and on, like is always in a still place. 'Surely to goodness I'll rest me here,' I said, and I lay me down. Jesus came. He came from behind me somewheres. Me so humble in sin I never looked up after the first sight, or lifted up my eyes. 'Preach my gospel,' he says. Jesus spoke. So still you could hear a pin fall. And I says: 'What'll I preach?'

"It was a long while I waited for the next, and then Jesus spoke again, in whisper. 'Open the Book!' he says. 'Preach,' says he, 'where the book falls open.'

"Humble in sin I was, and bent to the floor. I crawled over the floor on my hands and knees and lay on my belly to cry: 'God ha' pity on me,' and my tears ran like rain. Finally I came slowly up into the pulpit and I raised me up and opened the Book. You could hear a pin drop whilst I opened the Book. It falls open on Genesis, and the first line my eye lights on is 'Seedtime and harvest, and cold and heat, and summer and winter, and day and night shall not cease.'

"Then I looked to see what Chapter that would be and I saw the Eighth and near the end. And I read forward, before and after. But these are the words Jesus spoke to me in Fairhope Church. . . ."

His voice fell away to a whisper and he closed his eyes, his smile at the left of his mouth. While he waited, his hand still outstretched, Dickon began to speak above him:

"Hera, the atmosphere that surrounds the earth, there you've got the source of all vegetative life. Ethereal seed, life for the planet. Productive principles. Ether, the pure invisible fire. You've got Hera and Zeus. Sluttish stories to tell you the truth. What's mankind but one atomic stench in the multiplied system. Cools off your pride to know what a minute atomic particle mankind is in front of all these Causes. Hah, hah, hah! Knocks your big-mouthed pride south-east-north and again. Hera, source of vegetative stuff. Vegetative then produces animal. All said then."

The preacher spoke again, brushing the air with his hand as if he brushed aside a fly that troubled him. He took forward his sermon, preaching formally, addressing Drake:

"Forward and backward, I learned the words. 'And they went in unto Noah into the ark, two and two of all flesh, wherein is the breath of life. And they that went in, went in male and female of all flesh, as God had commanded him: and the Lord shut him in. And the flood was forty days upon the earth; and the waters increased, and bare up the ark, and it was lift up above the earth. And the waters prevailed, and were increased greatly upon the earth; and the ark went upon the face of the waters. And the waters prevailed exceedingly upon the earth; and all the high hills that were under the whole heaven, were covered. Fifteen cubits upward did the waters prevail; and the mountains were covered. And all flesh died that moved upon the earth, both of fowl, and of cattle, and of beast, and of every creeping thing that creepeth upon the earth, and every man: all in whose nostrils was the breath of life, of all that was in the dry land, died. And every living substance was destroyed which was upon the face of the ground, both man, and cattle, and the creeping things, and the fowl of the heaven; and they were destroyed from the earth: and Noah only remained alive, and they that were with him in the ark. And the waters prevailed upon the earth an hundred and fifty days.

" 'And God remembered Noah, and every living thing, and all the cattle that was with him in the ark: and God made a wind to pass over the earth, and the waters assuaged; the fountains also of the deep and the windows of heaven were stopped, and the rain from heaven was restrained; and the waters returned from off the earth continually: and after the end of the one hundred and fifty days the waters were abated. And the ark rested in the seventh month, on the seventeenth day of the month, upon the mountains of Ararat. And the waters decreased continually until the tenth month: in the tenth month, on the first day of the month, were the tops of the mountains seen. And it came to pass at the end of forty days, that Noah

opened the window of the ark which he had made: and
he sent forth a raven, which went forth to and fro, until
the waters were dried up from off the earth. . . .' "

"Not one god in all ever took notice to mankind. Fits
into the scheme, he does. Takes his place and no more
said."

" 'Sent forth a raven, which went to and fro, until the
waters were dried up from off the earth. . . .' "

"All life shut inside the will of Jupiter. Back you go
then, his mother, Rhea, and her father, Chronos, Time,
they called 'im, and he was the son of Terra. You're back
now to Chaos."

"That's all. Jesus spoke to me. In Fairhope Church on
a hot day in July, me so steeped in sin my mind was full
to run over with sluttish songs I'd learned the night before
from Amos Nick and Lilly Bannon. 'Preach my gospel,'
Jesus says to me. 'What gospel will I preach?' I says, two
sluttish songs a-beaten time in my mind even whilst I
spoke to my Lord Jesus. 'Open the Book!' he says to me.
That's all. We could sing now a hymn. . . ."

"Hah, hah, hah! Cares not so much as your dirty shirt
whe'r he sinks or swims or some other."

"I tell you, God shut Noah inside the ark," Briggs called
out.

"Shut nobody."

"You call me a lie," Briggs said to him, his hand up-

236

lifted, "and I'll punch your head against I catch you outside the house tomorrow."

Dickon began to laugh. "You are a strong man, Jack Briggs, but tiresome. With all your strength you never yet fought but one fight and that with Rafe Fowler. And he knocked you silly with a wrench. Take that." He slapped Briggs with the back of his hand.

Briggs leaped forward and grappled at the other's shoulders and beat three blows upon his head. Dickon grappled at Briggs's throat but lost his hold and flung out a boxer's blow at his chest, trampling at the same time the other's bare feet with his rough brogues. Briggs cried out at this last hurt and hurled himself at Dickon with renewed strength. Their swaying bodies brushed the table aside and Drake steadied the swaying lamp, calling out orders that were unheeded. The unheeded voice went as a threshing sound over the noise of blows and scuffling, of curse and threat and the rough breathing of straining bodies. Dickon beat blow after blow on the other's head, and the sound was that of hail beating the ground. The blood of Briggs's wounded foot ran to the floor and smeared in a broken arc. Then Drake leaped from his chair and entered the fight. With a great curse he flung himself upon the two that grappled together and he pressed Dickon back.

"Open the door," he called out to Briggs. "Out there! Outside, you, Dickon, you dirty varmint."

The door open, the two of them thrusting together, Drake and Briggs, and Dickon was pressed over the threshold. As he passed he tried to drag Drake with him, but Drake held his footing and Briggs, having got his breath anew, thrust forward with both arms and pushed the other quite beyond the door-frame. The door was quickly shut and the key turned.

"Go stay the night with the Tobins, if they'll have you," Drake called through the shut door. "If they won't take you in, go up to the far cabin. You can crawl in with Stump."

Briggs and Drake stood, breathing heavily from the exertions of the fight. "Void space, I'll hear no more of it," Drake muttered, shuddering with his heavy breath, "I'll hear it no more." Briggs trailed blood wherever he stepped, for his feet were bruised and the skin torn. Then Drake took a clean cloth from the sideboard at the south wall of the room and he poured a little wine from the squat jug into a cup. He gave these things to Briggs and told him he might wipe the blood away, saying that the wine would cleanse his sores.

Drake built up the fire with a quantity of coal from a hod on the hearth, and he stirred the burning mass until the flame went white and red into the chimney. Then he reseated himself in his chair near the east wall. Briggs took

238

the cup toward the fireplace and he dipped a corner of
the napkin into the wine and brushed it lightly over his
insteps, cleansing away the blood. He wiped his hands
on the cloth, freeing them of blood and dust, and he set
the cup well back on the hearth and put the cloth beside it
rolled into a little sheath. He walked slowly up and down
the room. He set the lamp straight on the sideboard and
he turned the wick up and down until it made a more
even light. He gathered a litter of papers that had been
thrown to the floor and put it straight on the table. Walking slowly, putting order about him, he came at length to
stand in the floor before Drake, near the middle of the
room, and he said:

"Stoner Drake, I've come to preach you salvation. It's
been long enough I've said no word to you. Tonight I told,
before the blasphemer fought me, how I saw Jesus. Jesus
spoke to me. It was years ago. I was a man of sin. Drink
and women were my kind. I never robbed a man. I lied
a heap to cover up my sin. I let my old mammy go cold
and hungry. Drunk, and I didn't know whe'r she had food
to eat or not or firewood to warm her. I already told how I
began to preach.

"With his own hand God shut Noah inside the ark.
You took notice to that."

"I did," Drake said.

"God shut Noah inside the ark. With his own hand he
closed the door to make all safe against the flood."

"Yes, sir. It's written plain."

"But God let Noah find his own way out, you understand. The waters ceased. God made a wind to pass over the earth and the waters assuaged, the fountains of the deep and the windows of heaven were stopped and the rain from heaven was restrained. End of forty days, and Noah himself opened the window. Old Noah had to find his own way out. Ark at rest now. Tops of the mountains in plain sight. All inside the ark have got to do for themselves now. First thing out is a raven, and he goes to and fro, to and fro, over the void. Next he sends out a dove from him, to see if the waters are abated, gone down, that means, from off the face of the ground, but the dove found no rest for the sole of her foot, and Noah put forth his hand and took her and brought her in unto himself into the ark. She told what Noah wanted to know. Mankind, it's like I say."

A faint voice came from above, down the hallway, crying: "You preach Ararat and no more. A little Sinai, you preach, and Ararat. Preach him now the Redeemer."

"Who spoke there?"

"Preach the Redeemer. Martha said it. Preach the Redeemer."

"I know that my Redeemer liveth."

"Preach him."

There was a pause in the discourse, the house quiet. Then Briggs lifted his gaze from the floor and made an upward gesture with his palm.

"I can preach only what Jesus told me. 'Open the Book!' he said to me in Fairhope Church. It was a Thursday, I recollect. And I opened, and I saw forward and back, as I already told. 'While the earth remaineth, seedtime and harvest, and cold and heat . . .' Stoner Drake, you couldn't get shed of God's seedtime and harvest. You used God's cold and heat, God's summer and winter, God's day and night. You already used, like I say. Think you're off the earth, and God's own winter weather makes you sit by a fire in God's own night time. The wine from God's own harvest to warm your old blood. You blasphemed your own oath, you said sin to yourself with your own fist every time you beat your oath out on a table top, and you sinned against your own word and took your own damnation on yourself. Put curses on yourself with your own mouth and went counterwise to your own hand that lifts up to take food into your mouth, and the food ought to choke the breath out of your maw, but God is merciful, you sinner against your own."

He leaned forward and whispered in a loudly breathed speech that came slowly from his large mouth, and he bent forward nearer, making the words stand apart, one from the next.

"Find your salvation before it's too late, Stoner Drake. Mend what you hurt. Seek your salvation."

"What will I do?" Drake asked. He leaned forward from his chair, pushing back at the arm-pieces. "What will I do?"

"Go first out into the outside and grapple up the dirt of a field in your hands. Pick up the dirt of anywhere in your fingers. Go out where the cattle are. Go where you grew corn. Go outside your land and along the road, quiet, a little at a time, not to make a show. Go east past Hood's and Stanley's and on further, and come on a day of worship to the little church on the hill above Simpson's Run, Bethel, they call the place. Mankind, go inside and shout and sing with all there, and praise God, and kneel down on the hemp carpet and beat your fists on the floor and cry out: 'God have mercy,' with all the rest there, men and women.

"Or go some other way till you come to McEllery's or Captain's or Bush's, a little at a time and no show of what you do, past Clover's Creek and on, west or south, and you'll come to another, on a hill above Wheelwright's Creek. Crawl inside the door over the wood floor and you'll see up above a little light always there, and people inside on their knees. Crawl to a back pew somewhere and get on your knees with the rest. Down beyond all the people you'll see the altar and you'll see the image of the blessed Mother, Mary, and you'll see Joseph, Father of Jesus, and

242

the priest will cry out in a tongue you'll know because you're a learned man. Get on your knees in the dust with all the balance and say in whisper outen the dust of your heart when the others say it: 'Lord have mercy, Christ have mercy, Lord have mercy.' "

"Get back off me," Drake cried out. "Stand back. Get back and away."

"I'll say through to the end, now I'm begun. Mankind, you hear what I say, sinner that I was, but a hope now inside my heart."

"Get back off me with your words. See't you get back and away now."

"I'm back. There's one thing more, man, and you'll hear me while I say it and you can't help the power of hearen God himself put into your ears. I see a sign. I see a prophecy. Days go by. Old Stoner Drake keeps fast shut his heart against mankind and never stopped to know he's mankind himself and beholden to God for whatever pleasure he's got, no matter how little. Days go by. One day the house goes up in flames. Nobody here to drag old Drake outside. Fire roars down from the roof and fire roars up from the floor. Red flames and black smoke and bitter fumes. Old Drake blows loud on his horn but nobody is there to hear. Put out the fire! Where's Martha? Where's Jocelle? Blows a loud roar on his horn. Rings his farm bell. Nobody comes that way. Everybody gone. Red fire runs through all the house. The roof about to fall in.

He goes out on the bridge. Fire all around, over the cabin, over the bridge that's about to fall down in red embers.

"People come. The flames drive a man back if he comes near. Then two run up into the smoke and fire, and they put a ladder up against the bridge. 'Come down, old man,' they say. 'While it's yet time, come down!' He wants to come. God knows he does, but he won't do it. Wants to, but he can't. He roars anger at the fire, anger at God. He screams and yells. He runs back into the burning. Let us pray."

Drake arose from his place and took the lamp from the sideboard, moving swiftly and firmly. He waved Briggs aside. "Get back off me," speaking sharply. "Get away." He walked out at the door, going toward his sleepingroom, and his step was quick and sharp in the hallway.

After the silence of the prayer, Martha called in a spent voice from above the stairway: "It's late now. I can't come down. See to the fire, Jack. Cover it with the dead ash. In the parlor, cover that, if there's any left. Make it safe for the night."

Jocelle was there, and she was gone or back again, scarcely realized as absent, for her thought of Martha did not cease and her will toward Martha was felt in the continual care that kept the fire all day in Martha's grate and brought the needed things to her couch. Nettie Tobin

244

being directed by letter or by telephone if Jocelle were away. Two months thus, and then she was more continually at hand, Logan gone far to try to contrive something for himself. Or back again, in the lower west chamber to stay his allotted hour. He would not stay longer, and he would not come to Drake's table. He was swift, coming leaping over the spring grass, up the stairs to greet Martha, and then with Jocelle out into the pasture before the house where the water of the pond lapped in spring against the higher stones of the fill and where the lambs and the ewes sometimes grazed. Or he would come after nightfall, tapping at the window, as if he took part in a forbidden love. A great disaster had begun to sweep the country. Farms were being bought and sold at prices far in excess of those which the returns from the crops would now justify. The war-madness had come into the fields. From farm to farm, there was now too much yield, too many stock animals, too many plowed fields. Men were assuming debts they could never pay, were losing their land swiftly, swept on by the madness of buying and selling and driven by agents and speculators and lenders. The madness seemed without end. The cataclysm that had centered at Wolflick seemed now to have spread outward into every surrounding mile, and Jocelle looked abroad over the country in Logan's look, seeing what he saw. Near at hand, among their neighbors, there were debts for farm machinery which had been bought at a high market, the plunder now rusting unused, the debts drawing interest from the spent homesteads.

John Thomas had come back. He had not been sent overseas. He came to share with Drake in the sheep, as formerly, to share now in the growing crops. Drake walked slowly through the hallways and out to the bridge to cry orders to his hands in a thin voice. "Ruin to the land," he would be whispering as he walked. Tobin was gone.

"He'd drain my fields of their last strength," Drake said. "I know his kind. Stay until the land's worn out and move on to drain another. . . ."

The Tobins being gone, man and woman, Jocelle brought a woman, Stump's wife, whose name was Arlet, to help with the work of the kitchen and the house, and she brought the two, Stump and Arlet, to live in the near cabin, the ancient house of the Ainsleys. The crying of Arlet's infant wakened a sweet, swift pang in her thought, and she would run to comfort it or send Arlet to find out what might trouble.

Logan was back from his distant journey, or gone again, back to the west room, or driving with Jocelle along the summer highways. He had taken back his small farm when the succession of buyers abandoned the obligation, and he lived there with the laborers who would share in the yield of the fields. He was elusive, reaching through the land, a scheme, a plan, an idea, an ideal. Jocelle was hearty, living from hour to hour between these two, the one man

246

shut into the house and the other shut out of it. She grew her fowl in the run of the war-chickens, the same white breed as formerly. The horn still called her, but it blew less frequently. There was less to command.

"What will we name our child?" she asked Logan. They were happy in secret in their hours together.

"Name her, if it's a girl, name her Roxanna."

"Roxie Treer! The girls at the seminary will call her. 'I'll take Roxie Treer!'"

"And they'll take a good player. Whatever the game is."

They laughed together. She was remembering Patterson, the cheer leader, and she laughed again, looking outward with misty eyes.

"But if it's a boy, you can name it," he said.

"It'll be Ben, or maybe Stoner. We'll see. Ben Stoner."

But Drake's hand was often doubled into a fist that beat on the rail of the stair as he passed. He would mend his shoes, sitting on the sunny bridge in the autumn, and he mended for Jocelle, or for Stump and Arlet. The work done, he would sit bowed before the fire, neglectful of his ease, his clothes worn and ragged. "Call the roll of the rich!" he would cry out suddenly.

"Call the roll of the rich!" he cried from the bridge, looking out over his sparse barnyards. The surplus earned from the sales of the war crops was lost as loans unpaid or it had gone to pay for the implements bought, to pay taxes. Logan had taken his papers from Jocelle's hands. Amend-

247

ing or readjusting his sequences, he would be under the tree beyond the pond, or gone, or back to give the papers again to her keeping.

J.T. came in from the fields at three o'clock. It was autumn, the harvest not abundant, the tobacco coarsened by too many late rains. He passed Jocelle where she shelled corn in the runway of the east stable, where she turned the hand-mill that sent the grains of the maize in a flying fringe from the spout to fall into her basket. He stopped and laughed a mirthless laugh, looking at the hand that worked the crank of the mill.

"And when the child is born, will you dare leave it in the house when you go outside?"

"I'll take it in my arms, maybe. Carry her on one arm. I can do a heap with one hand free."

"And you'll lock tight your door at night. What for?"

"It's no matter what I do inside my own place. See what doors you'll lock when you get a baby of your own."

"It's a sinking ship," he answered her.

"Sink or not. Roxanna and her mammy are both good swimmers. Or, Ben, if it's Ben . . ."

"You better believe what I tell you."

"I believe. God knows how I believe. As long as the old tug floats, I'll stay aboard though. And swim after."

He went toward the house and in at the west door. Later, Jocelle heard him in his room above the diningroom pulling a drawer from the chest or flinging a bag from the closet. He would be preparing to leave. Gone, there would be but herself left to go freely in and out of the house, and to come into it. On the lookout above Drake watched the drag-slides taking the tobacco from the old west field to the tobacco barn. J.T. was gone there later, and a storm of argument arose, a last demand. Right and wrong were bent and twisted, two-ways and back, both men claiming all the arguments and each giving the other unreason. J.T. was unwilling to take his loss, wanting the farm sold that he might be paid in full. Jocelle was thinking that, J.T. gone, perhaps she would bring Stump and Arlet to sleep somewhere in the house. Drake remained on the bridge until the dusk had fallen darkly, until the last load of the tobacco was housed and the mules were brought to the stable. Passing from her room, the west chamber below stairs, going to prepare the supper, Jocelle met J.T. in the hallway.

"It's a sinking ship. I'm leaving tonight."

"I'll be sorry to have you gone, but no matter . . ." And then she added bitterly: "It's said the rats leave a ship that's sinking. The rats leave it . . ."

"I'm gone for good, forever. You needn't say I didn't warn you. You needn't call me back."

"I'll never call you. I'll manage very well. Locked doors no matter. I'll stay with our own."

"We'll keep our land," Drake said to her. Or calling her with the horn, bringing her from the stables or the hen-runs.

"Jocelle, we'll keep our land."

"Our home, yes. We'll keep it."

"Jocelle."

"Oh, yes, we'll hold it."

"Bought already twice and won once in battle with the aborigines. Bought by the Ainsleys and paid for with continental money and with axes, cleared the soil of the trees. Paid for again by the Drakes."

From every side the house seemed to sleep, as if it had awareness, as if it knew that some part of the war was over. Martha viewed the stars from her couch in mid-winter, seeing those that lay to the south, using a field glass. Logan had grown tranquil, but he was swift in his coming.

The intolerable wrongs of the war past were not clearly remembered. Drake walked slowly and he went up the stairs less often, went but once or twice a day. He would come to her as she worked in the kitchen, as she played a little at the piano, coming softly over the floor dragging his heels lightly as he stepped.

"We'll keep our land," whispering, as if it were a secret they held together.

"Yes, we'll hold it. Work for it again if we have to."

"Jocelle!"

"I'm here."

"What was the name of the woman?"

She did not know how to answer him. She found warm clothes for him and kept his fire glowing, calling Stump to bring the coal. Sitting before the flame in his accustomed place, he said to her one day:

"A house burned somewhere. Where was it? I can't remember."

"Was it close by?"

He said that it was but she could not answer him.

A spring came on swiftly. Jocelle leaned against the rail of the porch at the south and felt the house float and swim in its ocean of greenery. The birds were mad with life among the old trees about the house, and at evening the little screech-owl whimpered his strange song above the windows. She prepared the west room below for her lying-in. She took away the heavy draperies from the windows, faded brocades that had hung there since the time of Joan. "Above stairs with you," Drake said, looking in at the doorway. "I won't have a howling bastard brat in here." She went forward with what she did, moving slowly toward the final preparations. She laid a fire in the grate and put matches near at hand. "Call Stump," she said, and he went to the door and lifted the horn to blow the one long blast. "The Species Man, where is he?" Drake came back to ask her, but he spoke half in whisper. Her body answered him as she went about the room, saying: "Thus it will be . . . myself and my child . . . here, now . . . Stand away."

"He will come today to stay as long as we are here," she answered. He will stay here now, no matter. She was firm and sad in what she said. She was thinking: "The winds are blown. The storm is nearly passed by."

The child, a girl, was born in the night. In the drowsy hours that followed Jocelle pondered the child, and the life she had thus far lived, the end and the beginning, the flight of Catharine, the long outward flowing arc of Martha's calamities, and Logan—unremitting, uncaptured, and unhoused. She had drawn life out of Wolflick where a lonely tomb closed over, had closed over Drake years ago. She had been somehow essential to his life and his days. The calling horn . . . She thought these things over. She would not trust that the child should be laid beyond the circle of her arm. Sleeping, and waking, she saw within the act of seeing, as if the brain itself were a prism, a crystal-clear design, a mathematical form, and as such common to all men. Common-to-all-men drowsed over her and brought Logan from the garden where he now rested from the long night of sharing with her the coming of the child, where he sat within the reach of her calling, but she lay still, letting him rest. And thus, a clear design, the mind, common to all men, it pointed an index, to a communal sharing which was religious, the sharing of the common mental pattern where individual traits merged.

And therefore of fear and faith and praise.

In it somewhere or somehow came the Redeemer.

Under this again, under communal devotions and emotions, the lonely will, the wish, the desire (Drake, then, blowing his hoarse note on the bridge), the underlying complexity reducible within itself and of itself to the one simple determinate, lonely among its fellows, aloof, arising now to a super-life, the will to believe, to live, to hate evil, to gather power out of emotion, to divide hate from love where the two are interlocked in one emotion, the will to love God the Creator. She thought of these things.

Drake's step through the hall was light because she was reported to be sleeping. He did not call her on the horn. He would come to sit beside her after three or four days were past. She would take the child then to her arms. Or sitting later beside her window, holding the infant, he would come to her. She uncovered the small form for him to see.

"They are all like snakes," he said.

"Yes, like little sleeping reptiles. It's their relaxed quiet makes them seem so."

"What was the name of the woman?" he asked.

She did not know how to answer him. His eyes were clear and his face clear now, as lifted from his bent body, suddenly lifted, clear, looking aloft with sudden brightness.

"Was it Joan, the woman?"

He shook his head.

"The woman of your vow? It was Joan."

"No, it was something else."

"Helen," she said. "Was it Helen Ware?"

"That was it. Helen. Her name was Helen."

"Can you remember Helen?"

He waited a little and he shook his head. "I can remember her hair. It was brown. She was little. You could pick her up with one arm. Helen, her name was."

"We'll give J.T. the land beyond the creek," she said. "Too much here, anyhow, for one man to care for right."

He nodded his head. She spoke again softly:

"It's good bottomland, thirty acres, and the rest fine upland, about ninety acres in all. He'll be glad to have it."

He nodded again.

"And this-side, about a hundred and thirty acres, for you and me and Martha—and Roxanna. Logan will manage it for us. He's a good hand with land. Knows soils. Knows sheep. He thinks we ought to rest the land."

He nodded again, his eyes bright.

"The land worn down. Worn away more than you

254

knew. Too many crops. We'll go back to sheep and cattle. Build up the soil. Two hundred sheep won't be too many for Wolflick. I'll ask Logan Treer to manage for us. I know he will."

He nodded his head, his eyes were still bright. His smile came and went, faintly moving his thin face. He walked back to the hearth and sat in his accustomed place.